"I can't believe I'm going to be a father to a little girl and boy. It's so unreal. And wonderful."

It was hard not to soften under the pride in his deep voice. She'd always loved Jace's voice, so warm and enveloping and inviting, especially when he whispered to her in the dark.

Sawyer sensed those days were long gone. Nothing could be the same now that they were married, and married under circumstances he'd no doubt come to regret one day. Speaking of regret, she figured she might as well put everything in the open now. She took a deep breath.

"Jace, here's the main reason you and I have a marriage that's probably going to be difficult. I know your family really never trusted mine."

"Sort of stating it too harshly," Jace said. "We didn't know what to think. Besides, we've put all that to rest with our marriage."

Dear Reader,

The final Callahan bachelor is about to fall, and the journey was so much fun to write! Was there ever a man more destined for love and family than Jace? And yet falling for one's neighbor—considered no friend of the family—can't be all that good an idea, can it? But Sawyer Cash has long been Jace's siren call—the petite, red-haired fireball tempts him madly! Sleeping with the enemy has never been so satisfying...until twin babies enter the picture. Double trouble!

What does a hunky cowboy do when everything he's ever wanted is on the wrong side of the fence? Jace will need all the mystical assistance Rancho Diablo has to offer if he's ever to win Sawyer Cash's heart.

I hope you enjoy Jace's story. And then, on to little sister Ash's own perilous trek to love.

Best wishes and happy reading always,

Tina

HER CALLAHAN
FAMILY MAN

—

TINA LEONARD

HARLEQUIN® AMERICAN ROMANCE®

Recycling programs
for this product may
not exist in your area.

ISBN-13: 978-0-373-75502-8

HER CALLAHAN FAMILY MAN

Printed in U.S.A.

ABOUT THE AUTHOR

Tina Leonard is a *USA TODAY* bestselling and award-winning author of more than fifty projects, including several popular miniseries for the Harlequin American Romance line. Known for bad-boy heroes and smart, adventurous heroines, her books have made the *USA TODAY,* Waldenbooks, Ingram and Nielsen BookScan bestseller lists. Born on a military base, Tina lived in many states before eventually marrying the boy who did her crayon printing for her in the first grade. You can visit her at www.tinaleonard.com, and follow her on Facebook and Twitter.

Books by Tina Leonard

HARLEQUIN AMERICAN ROMANCE

1129—MY BABY, MY BRIDE *
1137—THE CHRISTMAS TWINS *
1153—HER SECRET SONS *
1213—TEXAS LULLABY
1241—THE TEXAS RANGER'S TWINS
1246—THE SECRET AGENT'S SURPRISES**
1250—THE TRIPLETS' RODEO MAN**
1263—THE TEXAS TWINS
1282—THE COWBOY FROM CHRISTMAS PAST
1354—THE COWBOY'S TRIPLETS‡
1362—THE COWBOY'S BONUS BABY‡
1370—THE BULL RIDER'S TWINS‡
1378—HOLIDAY IN A STETSON
        "A Rancho Diablo Christmas"
1385—HIS VALENTINE TRIPLETS‡
1393—COWBOY SAM'S QUADRUPLETS‡
1401—A CALLAHAN WEDDING‡
1411—THE RENEGADE COWBOY RETURNS‡
1418—THE COWBOY SOLDIER'S SONS‡
1427—CHRISTMAS IN TEXAS
        "Christmas Baby Blessings"
1433—A CALLAHAN OUTLAW'S TWINS‡
1445—HIS CALLAHAN BRIDE'S BABY‡
1457—BRANDED BY A CALLAHAN‡
1465—CALLAHAN COWBOY TRIPLETS‡
1473—A CALLAHAN CHRISTMAS MIRACLE‡

*The Tulips Saloon
**The Morgan Men
‡Callahan Cowboys

Many thanks to the wonderful readers who have taken the Callahan family into their hearts—your enthusiasm has made their stories possible.

"The Callahans fight to win. They'd rather die than give an inch. And there's not an inch of quit in them."

—Neighboring ranch owner Bode Jenkins, when asked by a reporter why the Callahans simply didn't move away from Rancho Diablo

Chapter One

Jace Chacon Callahan stared back at the petite fireball glaring at him. Sawyer Cash was his nemesis, his nightmare, the one woman that could keep him awake at night, racked by desire. Her killer body and haunting smile stayed lodged in his never-at-rest brain. And now here she was, red hair aflame and blue eyes focused, oblivious to the fact that his mind was never quite free of her. "*You're* the bidder who won me at the Christmas ball?" Jace demanded.

Sawyer shrugged. "Don't freak out about it. Someone had to bid on you. I was just trying to contribute to your aunt Fiona's charity. Are we going to do this thing or not?"

He seemed to be locked in place, thunderstruck. For starters, Sawyer was telling a whopper of a fib. There'd been plenty of ladies bidding a few weeks ago for the chance of winning a dinner date with a Callahan bachelor, which happened to be him.

But what had him completely poleaxed was that the little darling who had such spunk—and whatever else you wanted to call the sass that made her an excellent bodyguard and a torture to his soul—was that Sawyer was quite clearly, this fine February day, as pregnant as a busy bunny in spring.

In a curve-hugging, hot pink dress with long sleeves and a high waist, she made no effort to hide it. Taupe boots adorned her feet, and she looked sexy as a goddess, but for the glare she wore just for him.

A pregnant Sawyer Cash was a thorny issue, especially since she was the niece of their Rancho Diablo neighbor Storm Cash. The Chacon Callahans didn't quite trust Storm, yet in spite of that fact they'd hired Sawyer to guard the Callahan kinder.

But then Sawyer had simply vanished off the face of the earth, leaving only a note of resignation behind. No forwarding address, a slight he'd known was directed at him.

Jace knew this because for the past year he and Sawyer had had "a thing," a secret they'd worked hard to keep completely concealed from everyone.

He'd missed sleeping with her these past months. Standing here looking at her brought all the familiar desire back like a screaming banshee.

Yet clearly they had a problem. Best to face facts right up front. "Is that why you went away from Rancho Diablo?" he asked, pointing to her tummy.

She raised her chin. "Are we going on this date or not? Although it won't surprise me if you back out, Jace. You were never one for commitment."

Commitment, his boot. Of his six siblings, which consisted of a sister and five brothers, he'd been the one who'd most wanted to settle down, maybe even return to his roots in the tribe. By now he'd been fighting the good fight for Rancho Diablo for such a long time he never thought about living anywhere but here, or at least no farther away than the land across the canyons, which his brother Galen had shocked them all by acquiring, in a direct assault on Aunt Fiona's marriage raffle for the property.

The siblings thought Galen had cheated, or at least "rigged" the ranch deal in his favor. Jace and Ash hadn't had a chance to marry and have babies, all prerequisites for Fiona's ranch raffle. Ash was still steamed as heck with her big brother, Galen, whom she adored—although not when it came to acquiring the ranch she'd already named Sister Wind Ranch, which was actually called Loco Diablo by him and his brothers.

Jace wanted the land for himself, but he'd never pushed hard enough to find a lady with whom he could settle down and start a family, a necessary component of the marriage raffle. He'd been too busy chasing Sawyer night and day—or, to be more precise, letting himself get caught by her.

He gazed at her stomach again, impressed by the righteous size to which she'd grown in the short months since he'd last seen her—and slept with her.

He wished he could drag her to his bed right now.

"I'm your prize, beautiful," he said. "No worries about that. But before we go, you're going to admit whether that child you're carrying is mine or not." He wouldn't be able to eat a bite, thinking about another man finding his way into Sawyer's sweet bed. Jace broke into an uncomfortable sweat just imagining someone else with his adorable darling.

"I'm hungry, and in no mood to chat." Sawyer turned to walk away, and he caught her hand to stop her, pulling her toward him. That she was avoiding the topic told him everything he needed to know.

"It's my baby," he stated quietly, his gaze pinning hers. "Don't deny it."

"I'm not."

Her perfume wrapped around him; her heart-shaped lips were close enough to kiss. His ears rang with her admission, and Jace struggled to take in that he'd awakened this frosty February morning in Diablo, New Mexico, a free man—and would go to bed a caught man, and a father. "You're having my baby?"

She gazed at him with those blue eyes that had long intoxicated him, even though he knew she was sexy trouble. "I'm having your *babies*."

If he hadn't been such a strong person, a man of steel forged by fire, as he frequently told himself, he'd have raised an eyebrow with surprise. *"Babies?"*

"Twins. One boy, one girl, if the doctor's correct."

Stunned was too gentle a word for the emotion searing him. The vixen who'd avoided him these past four months, not even letting him know where she was—who'd made him believe he was never going to hold her in his arms again—was the sin to which he was now tied.

His family was going to razz him a good one—and they weren't going to toss confetti in congratulations. They'd say he'd gone over to the dark side, had slept with the enemy's niece.

Hell, yeah, I did. And she's having my children.
I'm on top of the world, even if I'm going to Hell.

SAWYER CASH GREW wary as the handsome cowboy she'd spent months dreaming about steered her toward his truck. She didn't like the sudden glint in his eye when he'd realized she was pregnant with his children—and she knew the Callahans well enough to know that a glint in the eye meant their wild side was kicking in. "Where are we going?"

"On the date you bid for and won, darling. Be a lamb and hop in my truck," Jace said, opening the door for her.

She'd always love the wild in Jace Chacon Callahan. His eyes were that navy color all the Callahan men had, but his were both a little distant and a little crazy. His hair was always tousled, dark strands going haywire except when tamed by a cowboy hat. Even his laugh was a bit wild, tinged with the devil-may-care attitude that most of the Callahan men possessed.

She'd always been attracted to Jace—but right now he made her nervous.

"Since I won you, I get to pick the date parameters, right? I mean, I paid for something."

He smiled, slow and sexy, heating her with memories of snatched passion they should never have shared. "Whatever you want, little darling. Now slide in so I can buckle you up good and tight."

Warnings howled in her psyche. She didn't like anything about his sudden determined mood. "There's a cute little restaurant in Tempest we could check out."

"Tempest." He buckled her in with care and stared into her eyes, just inches from her face. "It's a funny thing, but the night of the Christmas ball, all I learned about the woman who won me was that she was from Tempest."

"At the time I bid, I was working for your brother Galen in Tempest," she said, a little breathless at the devilish look in Jace's eyes. "At Sheriff Carstairs's place. You know about what happened there."

He had to have heard about the night Sawyer and her cousin Somer had taken shots at each other, quite by accident. Hired by Galen, Sawyer had been doing her job—

and Jace hadn't had any idea she was only a short truck ride away in Tempest, which was how she'd wanted it.

All the same, it had been hard not to drive "home" to Rancho Diablo to see him. But she'd known that to see Jace meant falling under his spell and into his arms.

She'd done far too much of that. Obviously.

"You covered your tracks real well." He checked her seat belt again and she smacked his hand away, making him laugh in a throaty, teasing growl. He was just itching to get on her nerves in every way, and he was certainly succeeding. "Disappeared for months, then took a job with Galen, which I consider a bit traitorlike on your part. Then deliberately won me at Aunt Fiona's auction. As I recall, the bidding went sky-high that night. I, the last Chacon Callahan bachelor to be on the block, fetched the highest price ever. Which you paid, and no one twisted your arm at all."

She couldn't look away from the knowing laughter in his eyes. "You're a bit of an ass, Jace."

"Yes, ma'am." He closed the door, went around to the driver's side. She could hear him guffawing with delight at her admission that she wanted him.

Well, she *had* wanted him, and she *had* paid a record amount for him at the Christmas ball, determined that no other woman should win him that night, not when she'd just learned she was pregnant. Five thousand dollars had gone to Fiona's favorite charity, thanks to her sexy nephew. Jace's aunt had no idea how many times Sawyer had fallen under Jace's spell, seduced by the hot cowboy with a wicked penchant for frequent, enthusiastic lovemaking.

She couldn't even comfort herself with the thought that he was a dud of a lover, or lacked the skills or attributes a female adored. No, he was pretty much perfect as a lover. And darn well aware of it, too. "So, we'll head to Tempest for dinner?"

He started the truck, pulled out from the driveway at Rancho Diablo, where she'd agreed to meet him as his mystery date. "Sure, we can eat there. But not tonight. Tonight, we're going to take a romantic drive." He glanced over at her. "You cute little thing, trying to sneak up on me with this surprise pregnancy. You didn't have to win me at the auction just to tell me about the babies. I would've married you even if you hadn't bid for me. You could have had me for free."

He was so arrogant! "I did not want, and do not want, to marry you. Put that right out of your insane mind."

Apparently Jace thought her words were a real thigh-slapper. Sawyer's brows drew together in a frown as he laughed. "Something funny?" she asked.

"Reverse psychology is an excellent tool." He glanced over and stroked her cheek. "You didn't pay five grand just to have dinner with me, doll face."

He was insufferable. Why had she bothered to try to keep another woman from getting her manicured hands on him?

Sawyer should have thrown him to the wolves with a smile on her face.

"Jace, tonight is about dinner only. I've lived without you just fine for the first several months of this pregnancy, and I can continue to do well on my own. I suggest you try to grasp that. While you and I may have some parenting details to work out, there'll be no resumption of our former relationship."

"Could you classify that former relationship for me?"

He was definitely digging down to find his deepest

layer of smart-ass. "Working professionals with benefits. You know that as well as I."

"And now that you're pregnant, those benefits are no longer beneficial?"

She could hear the smirk in his voice. "That's right."

He hit the main road, but they weren't heading for Tempest. "I believe you went the wrong way," Sawyer stated.

"I'm going the only way we need to go," Jace said. "You and I are taking a side trip to Vegas. We're going to give my children my name. Then if you want to sleep alone, that's your choice. I won't fight you about that. But being a father to my children, Sawyer, I will fight for." He glanced at her, his smile slightly amused. "I'm a pretty good fighter."

She knew that. All the Callahans were stubborn, steeped in loyalty to family and land. It was one of the reasons she'd fallen in love with Jace. Now he wanted to marry her, have a quickie wedding to seal the torrid love affair they'd shared under the family radar. She was a Cash and he was a Callahan, and the two were never supposed to meet on more than a professional basis.

"We can do this without marriage," Sawyer said a bit desperately as he sped toward Vegas. "We can divide custody with the use of legal instruments instead of a marriage ceremony."

"We've come this far, we may as well go all out. My family's going to flip out when they find out I've…" He hesitated, then glanced at her with a grin. "That I'm having children."

"That you've impregnated the enemy?" She glared at him. "I can't think of a worse reason to get married."

"I can't, either, but we're apparently past needing a

reason and are moving swiftly on to cause. Those children deserve a proper start in life. That's all there is to this, Sawyer Cash. Don't feel guilty because you've worked your wiles on me, and are finally getting what you wanted all along, when you made your way into my bed."

"*Not* your bed." Not with the furtive lovemaking they'd enjoyed. There'd been nothing traditional about their stolen moments together.

"Doesn't matter if it was truck bed, front seat, barn, canyon or Rancho Diablo roof. We misused ye olde condom somehow, and now the piper must be paid."

She rolled her eyes. "About that time on the roof…"

"You said you wanted to see the stars. I believe we achieved your goal."

He really was an insufferable jackass, quite confident that his lovemaking was the end-all to a woman's dreams, the gold buckle of mind-blowing sex.

She couldn't argue the point. She'd left Rancho Diablo when she'd realized she'd fallen head over heels in love with him, and that he had zero desire for a serious romance between them. He'd never said it in so many words, but she knew the difficulty of their relationship as well as anyone.

She'd thought she was in the clear, had made her escape with her pride intact. And then the morning sickness had begun.

"I don't want to get married, Jace."

"It's not about you. It's about our children. Now try to get some rest. There's a blanket in the backseat if you want it. When you awaken, it'll be time for us to find the fastest house of I do in Vegas."

Great. That sounded like a wedding she could always

look back on with a fond smile. No magic wedding dress for her, no marriage at the beautiful seven-chimneyed mansion at Rancho Diablo like all the other Callahan brides.

Drat. I had to fall for the one Callahan for whom a quickie, no-strings-attached marriage is just ducky.

Sawyer pulled the blanket over herself and closed her eyes so she wouldn't think about what she'd done, blowing her entire bank account on the wildest, wooliest Callahan of all. When she'd known quite well that the Callahans and the Cashs were never, ever going to trust each other.

Babies notwithstanding.

Chapter Two

"It does trouble me that you felt like you had to win me to have this conversation," Jace told Sawyer an hour later, as he sped toward Las Vegas. "I'm flattered you spent several months of your Rancho Diablo salary keeping me from another woman, but I would have withdrawn myself from Aunt Fiona's bachelor raffle if I'd known I was a father."

He looked over at Sawyer, noting that the spicy redhead looked as if she wanted to give him a piece of her mind, and probably would in a moment. He remembered the first time he'd ever laid eyes on her. Galen and he had played backup to Dante when he went over to see Storm Cash, and Sawyer had opened the door instead of her uncle, catching all of them off guard. Jace had seen a big smile, a slender, athletic body, cute freckles across a tiny nose, big blue eyes twinkling at him, and felt himself fall into deep, fiery lust—lust so strong that every time he saw her, he wanted her.

Of course, he'd known better. There were some lines one could cross, but sleeping with the enemy was a mistake only a man with his mind anywhere but on his job would make. But then she'd been hired on at Rancho Diablo by his brother Sloan and Sloan's wife, Kendall—and suddenly the red-hot neighbor sex-bomb was in Jace's sights like a tornado he couldn't avoid.

It hadn't taken him long to respond to the magnet pulling him toward Sawyer—only to discover that she seemed to feel the same desire. They'd made love as often as possible, as discreetly as possible, keeping their affair completely locked away. Sawyer didn't want to jeopardize her job, knowing that she still had to earn Callahan trust—and Jace hadn't wanted his family harping on his lack of loyalty.

His family was in for a big shock, but right now, he had to make certain his little firecracker mama got to the altar.

One thing about the Callahans: they were deadly serious about their ladies once they found them. But rare was the Callahan bride who'd made her way to the altar quietly.

He intended to avoid that unnecessary heartburn.

"I did not," Sawyer said with annoyance, "want you to withdraw from Fiona's event. You'd been advertised on barn roofs and billboards for months as Diablo's prize of the century. It wouldn't have been right to tell you at Christmas that you were going to be a father, and make you withdraw. That would have devastated Fiona, taken all the fun out of the Christmas ball and denied the charities that she funds much needed revenue, which comes from the purses of women who are hoping to win the dream man lottery."

Jace perked up at the idea that Sawyer might think he was a dream man, suddenly hopeful that shoehorning her into marrying him would be simpler than it had first seemed. She didn't appear all that anxious to say I do.

Unaware of his hopeful state, Sawyer took a deep

breath and stated, "I took care of the obvious problem of my children's father hanging out with another woman simply by winning you. It wasn't that big of a deal, Jace."

"You cute little thing." He smiled at her, impressed by the starch in her attitude. "I'm not going to lie and say that I'm not thrilled to find out you're my mystery girl. I'll be happy to put a ring on your finger tonight, Sawyer." And then, if good fortune smiled on him, maybe after the I dos were said, he'd finally get his little darling into a real bed, in a room with a closed door that locked, so he could enjoy her for hours on end.

"It's going to feel great not to rush things anymore," he said, not really aware he was speaking out loud, and Sawyer said, "I feel pretty certain we're rushing marriage. Marriage is the one thing in life that shouldn't be rushed at all."

"Well, that cow is long out of the barn, so we won't worry about that. Let's move on to big decision number two."

"I'm not even sure I want to be a Callahan," Sawyer said. "I think I'll keep my maiden name."

He nearly stomped on the brakes. "That's not going to happen, sweet cheeks. You and I are going to be Mr. and Mrs. Callahan, just like all my brothers and their wives. We share the children, we share the last name."

She sent him a frown. "I'm not persuaded."

"You will be. That's my gift, persuasion." He hoped she bought that corny line, and plowed on, "The second most important decision we make in life is where to live. I think the babies should be at the ranch, but everything's hot around there right now, as you know." They'd hired Sawyer in the first place because they'd needed bodyguards for the Callahan children. But later, they'd brought in more personnel to help keep Fiona and any other weaker links safe.

Of course, his redoubtable aunt would bean him a good one if she ever heard him refer to her as a weak link. But whether she liked it or not, she and Burke were getting up there in years.

"I can take care of myself. And the babies," Sawyer said. "It won't be much different from when I took care of Kendall's twins."

"I don't like it," Jace murmured, thinking out loud.

"No one asked you to like it."

"The problem is, bodyguards are supposed to be un-emotional about their assignment. You can't be unemotional about your own children. No, I'll have to look into hiring someone for you and the babies."

"No, you won't," Sawyer said, and it sounded as if she spoke through tightly clenched teeth. "I don't want a bodyguard. I'm not planning on living with you."

He checked her expression. Yep, she had that serious look on her face, and he recognized yet another hurdle in his relationship with the saucy redhead.

She didn't want him in her bed. That's what this was all about.

His wooing would have to be played very smoothly, because he absolutely would be in a real bed with Sawyer, undressing her, with a ceiling overhead and not the sky. He wanted to hold her in his arms and make her cry his name, without having to quietly rush through each and every encounter.

Sooner rather than later he intended to have his way with the beautiful bodyguard, sharing lovemaking that would be record-breaking in length and very, very satisfying. That was the plan for tonight—if he could figure out the key to the tight lock she was trying to keep on her heart.

Lucky for him, he was really good at picking locks.

THEY WERE HALFWAY across Arizona, halfway to Las Vegas and the Little Wedding Chapel, when Sawyer hit him with a bombshell.

"Several members of your family are on the way to witness our wedding."

To say his jaw dropped nearly to his lap would be putting it mildly. "My family?"

"Yes, and my uncle Storm, and his wife, Lulu Feinstrom." Sawyer beamed at Jace. "I know how your family loves a wedding, so I texted them. They'll be on the family plane soon and on their way, ready for wedding cake. At least that's what your sister said. Ash also mentioned she ordered us a whopper of a cake, because everyone in your family has had a sweet tooth since they were born. Her comment, not mine." Sawyer smiled, delighted that she'd outplayed him.

He'd seen her busily working on her phone, but he'd assumed she was looking up places to wed. Her decisive strategy meant Aunt Fiona and maybe even Uncle Burke were on their way. Jace knew he'd never get Sawyer into a bed for hours tonight, not with his partying family there. They'd want to kick up their heels and spend the evening giving him grief about how he'd surprised them with this sudden dash to the altar, blah, blah, blah, and they'd talk him to death, when he should be concentrating on undressing the redhead next to him.

It was really all he had on his mind.

Instead, he was going to get a whopper of a wedding cake.

"I don't have much of a sweet tooth," he said, casting a longing glance at her body in her hot pink dress. "I prefer spicier fare."

"I'll try not to feed you too big of a bite, then." She went back to texting, and he wondered if it was too late to text his family and explain that, while he loved them, he really wanted to handle this momentous occasion alone, because he was going to have a devil of a challenge getting his wife into a bed with him. He didn't have time for celebrating and family hijinks. Every second of his life until these babies were born had to be spent romancing his wife. After they arrived, he'd have precious little time alone with her, and he hadn't yet enjoyed his woman the way he wanted to.

He felt like a man who'd starved a long while in plain view of the most delicious meal he'd ever seen.

"It was nice of you to invite my relatives," he said, even though family was the last thing he wanted around.

"And mine," she said, her voice bright. "No bride wants to be married without someone to give her away."

There was the problem. His family and hers didn't get along, making the situation ripe for discomfort and fireworks.

"Anyway, I knew your family wouldn't want to miss the last Callahan bachelor getting married." Sawyer smiled at him, her big blue eyes completely innocent, when he knew that she was trying to put as much distance between them as possible.

"If we're going to marry, I want us to start out on the right foot with the in-laws and the outlaws," Sawyer said. "I wouldn't dream of leaving them out."

"Where are they booking rooms?" Jace asked.

"I don't know. But I'm booking us rooms at a bed-and-breakfast nearby."

He swallowed. "Rooms?"

She glanced up from the sudden storm of texts she was sending. "I meant room."

No, she hadn't. Jace could tell he was going to have to keep a very close eye on his little woman. No drinking too much and finding out she'd shuttled him into a room with his family. No visiting too much, or he'd probably find her headed back to Diablo without him. "Sex is what got us into this, darling."

"That's how it works," Sawyer said.

"Yet I have the strangest feeling you don't want to be alone with me."

"Callahans are known to have a lot of strange qualities. I wouldn't let it bother me now, if I were you."

"We'll stop and get you a ring," he said, giving up on sex for the moment.

"I don't need a ring. The vows are more than I want."

He grunted. "The ring is part of the ceremony. You'll have a ring."

"Are you going to wear one?"

He hadn't planned on it, but he sensed this was treacherous water. "Why wouldn't I?"

"I don't know." She ran a considering eye over him. "But if you are, I will."

"Back to our discussion of our domicile," he said.

"I'm planning on going to Rancho Diablo," Sawyer stated.

He blinked, hearing the thing he'd been sensing, the trouble at the end of the supposedly peaceful road. "Like, as soon as the 'I do' leaves your mouth?"

"Well, not until we've cut the cake." She looked at

him, puzzled. "Of course I plan to stay for the cake your sister ordered. It would be rude to leave!"

Great. Nothing said love like worrying about the sister's cake purchase. "I was thinking we'd live together."

"This morning, you didn't even know you were a father. So we don't have plans," Sawyer pointed out. "Spur-of-the-moment decisions are rarely a good idea."

"As in getting married in Vegas?"

"As in getting married in Vegas." She nodded. "I liked our relationship just the way it was."

He shook his head. "We didn't have a relationship. We had sex, but not a relationship."

She met his gaze. "Was there a problem?"

The problem had come when she'd left, and he realized he'd been parked at the gates of heaven for too long. Now he was hoping to crash through those gates and land in the paradise waiting for him—if he could just figure out how to explain that to Sawyer. How could a man tell his woman that, while frequent, horny sex had been fun, and fired by the forbidden, he sensed the next phase of their relationship could be that much sweeter?

Especially since she didn't seem inclined to recognize the possibility for an ongoing, more meaningful relationship between them.

"Not a problem, exactly," he said carefully. "But it seems that we should be open to the idea of a new phase in our friendship."

She didn't reply. "I know this pregnancy changes your life significantly," he added.

"Yes. It does." Sawyer turned her head to gaze out the window.

He had one reluctant little mama on his hands.

"Yours, too," she said. "I know the Callahans have a

pattern. You find out you're expecting, and immediately want to get married. Then the wife gets shuttled off to a safe location." Sawyer finally looked his way. "I'll expect you to treat our pregnancy differently."

"How differently?"

"By not trying to send me off to your family in Hell's Colony, or Tempest."

He swallowed. That had been the next plan. "The reason my brothers have been so determined for their wives and children to be in another location is because Rancho Diablo isn't safe. You know as well as anyone that my uncle Wolf has made things very difficult at the ranch. It's even worse now. Which is why your uncle Storm sold us his ranch and moved into town with Lulu Feinstrom."

"I'll be fine. I've already rented out a room from Fiona. Didn't she tell you? I called and asked her about renting a room before I came back to Rancho Diablo for our date. I do need a place to live now that my job in Tempest is completed."

"*You rented* a room?"

Sawyer nodded. "A marriage license won't mean I want to be a wife in anything other than name."

Well, there was nothing he could say to that. She'd ridden all over his poor flailing heart. It beat wildly in his chest, stressed and unhappy with his current circumstances.

There was only one thing to do.

He pulled over at the next rest stop and parked the truck. Then he pulled Sawyer close and laid a kiss to end all kisses on her. He didn't let her go, either, making certain she knew how much he desired her, kissing her long and thoroughly, communicating in a different way what he couldn't say out loud. And searching for that answer he wanted so badly: that she did, in fact, still want him.

It was a risky move, but when he felt her lips mold against his, Jace knew his belief in high risk, high reward had paid off.

His little darling still had the hots for him big-time— no matter how tightly she was trying to close those sweet, pearly gates.

SAWYER WAS SO annoyed with herself for giving in to Jace's charm that she sat stiffly staring out at the landscape rushing past. He'd caught her off guard, that was all. If she'd had a second's notice of his intention, she could have controlled her reaction better.

Jace drove down the road with a sexy, confident, "I win" curve to his lips, a true cat that ate the canary. Sharing that kiss was a huge setback to her plan, and devastating to her heart.

I promised myself that wouldn't happen. No more falling under his spell. Not one woman who married a Callahan kept her independence. It was as if they got their wedding ring and poof! instant Callahan copy. Babies and bliss.

Babies and bliss in every corner.

"I'm renting a room from Fiona because I'll be in Diablo only until the babies are born. Four months after that I'll be living in New York," Sawyer said.

That wiped the smirk off his face. "New York?"

"Yes. I've taken a job with a firm that provides security for high-profile clients."

"You're going to be a bodyguard while you should be staying at home with my children?" Jace shook his head. "I can see two big problems with your plan, doll face.

One, my children aren't going anywhere without me. Two, it's going to be terribly hard for you to be a home-room mother and a bake sale coordinator while you're working. My children need you more than high-profile clients do."

She stiffened. "I'm sure you're hoping I'll thank you for your opinion. However, I'm fully capable of making my own decisions."

"Yes, you are. And I trust you'll make decisions that are in the best interest of our family, not harebrained ones that are purely designed to keep you and me from sharing a bed."

He'd gotten pretty close to the truth. "That's not the reason I took the job, Jace. I'm a very good bodyguard, and there's still a lot I want to do and learn."

"Yes, but your days of living on the edge are over. You can get your fill of that at Rancho Diablo."

"So you'd be all right with me and the children living at Rancho Diablo?"

He hesitated. "I didn't exactly say that."

"Then we have nothing to discuss."

"We have plenty to discuss. And now that we've just passed the Nevada state line, we're getting closer to our destination, so I won't hesitate to mention that this is the happiest day of my life."

She gave him a curious glance. "Why?"

"It's not every day a man finds out he's going to be married and a father." He glanced at her. "Even better, that the woman who's providing all this excitement wanted him badly enough to pay five grand for him, thereby scuttling all other females' chances. Just so very cute of you." He laughed out loud, pleased with himself.

"You put up stop signs, but there's lots of green lights flashing all over you, Sawyer Cash."

He was angling for a good hard takedown to his ego. Sawyer told herself Jace had always been a goofball, and ignored him.

"Have you asked Galen to hire you on again at Rancho Diablo?" Jace asked, stunning her.

"No." Out of the corner of her eye, she saw him shrug.

"We're always looking for staff we can trust."

"Are you saying you trust me?" Sawyer asked.

"Are you insinuating I can't? Or shouldn't?"

His gaze met hers, and she found herself drawn in, the way he'd always drawn her in. With the memory of his hot kiss still warm on her lips, she'd be lying to herself if she tried to pretend she didn't want to experience once again what he could do with those wandering hands of his. Experience the sweet satisfaction of what miracles he worked with a mouth that never ceased talking smack, and the to-die-for sexy things he whispered to her during lovemaking.

But she couldn't allow herself to get caught in the snare of sex. The goal was far more important than the pleasure.

"I'm not insinuating anything. I don't want you and your family to give me busywork." Sawyer knew how this story would play out. The moon would be promised— and she'd wind up with nothing but a crash to earth. "I'm not the kind of woman who'll be happy staying home to wash your socks, Jace."

He laughed, and Sawyer favored him with a frown.

"My socks?" Jace chuckled again. "You have a problem with my socks?"

"I don't want to be a Callahan housewife. I intend to keep doing what I do."

"You're jumping the mark, sister. No one ever said you can't work. I encourage it."

"You do?"

"Sure thing." He grinned. "In fact, I'll stay home with the babies. How's that for a compromise?"

She blinked, not certain where he was going with that. While all the Callahan men stayed close to home once married, she didn't think Jace would be happy as a Mr. Mom while she earned the family bread. "You'll do diapers and bath time?"

"Sure." He shrugged, not fazed at all. "The babies will have organic food I prepare myself, too—none of that jar stuff. Baths with lavender oil, and a nightly de-stress rubdown. I'll sing lullabies and tell them stories I heard when I was a child in the tribe." He looked satisfied with that plan. "I'll have to see if Grandfather Running Bear can add to my collection."

"I don't believe a word you're saying."

He picked her hand up, brushed it against his lips. "Believe it. You work, and I'll be the best stay-at-home dad you ever saw."

"You're too much of a chauvinist, Jace."

"I resent that remark, darling. Don't you worry about a thing. This is going to work out so well, you'll wonder how you ever lived without me. Be the best five grand you ever spent."

She raised a brow. "That really wound your ego up, didn't it? Me spending that kind of money for a date with you?"

"Oh, angel." He kissed her hand again. "You paid that kind of cash for exactly what you're getting—a husband."

She sucked in a breath. "Jace, honestly, I don't know how you fit in this truck with your ego."

He laughed. "I bought the biggest truck I could."

There was nothing else to say to such enthusiastic patting of his own back. Anyway, she'd already gotten two concessions out of him: she could live at Rancho Diablo and she could keep her job.

His ego could take a flying leap.

Jace's phone buzzed. "Excuse me," he told Sawyer. "I have to take this." His gaze slid over to her as he pulled off the road so he could talk on the phone. "Hello, Grandfather."

Whenever Chief Running Bear spoke, everybody listened. The man said almost nothing unless it was important. Sawyer couldn't tell much of what was being communicated, but it was clear Jace's attention was clearly engaged.

"That's interesting news. I'll see what I can do."

He hung up, then steered the truck back onto the highway again. "Running Bear suggests we go into hiding immediately."

Sawyer gasped. "Hiding! Why?"

"Apparently Wolf's right-hand man, Rhein, was arrested today on suspicion of smuggling. This means the Feds have decided to clamp down on the illegal operations that are being run across the canyons. Running Bear says this will have the effect of ramping up Wolf's goal of taking over Rancho Diablo. He says that because of your pregnancy, it would probably be best. Wolf will post bail for Rhein soon enough, and no doubt the sheep will hit the fauna."

Sawyer shook her head at his attempt to be lighthearted about something that wasn't funny at all. "I'm not going into hiding."

"I thought you'd feel that way," Jace said. "We have another option."

She didn't smile at the devilish wink he sent her. "What option?"

"I'll guard you."

"You mean *I* would be assigned to you as a bodyguard," Sawyer said. "You have no experience."

He grinned. "However you want to play it, babe. I'd let you guard my body any day."

"It won't work. You wouldn't take it seriously." She shook her head. "Once I'm on bed rest, you'd drive me insane. The two of us working together would be an unfocused assignment." She thought about the babies, and what she would do once they were born. They'd be targets; they'd need special protection. She'd worked for the Callahans long enough to know that Running Bear's words were worth heeding. If he said that Rhein's arrest would add to the heat at Rancho Diablo, it couldn't be ignored. "If that was your only option, it wasn't a serious one."

"We're either on the road in hiding, or we stick together like glue. I guess it's going to depend on how you feel. When will the babies be born?"

"I'm five and a half months pregnant. I'm hoping to make it at least as far as April. But I know your sisters-in-law didn't carry their twins and trips quite as long as they would have liked. I'm in good shape, and the doctor says I'm on track for a normal pregnancy. So we'll see what happens."

"Okay. The goal is keeping you stress-free and resting. Hard to rest if you're on the run."

"Are we seriously talking about this?" She looked at him. "It's not in me to be afraid."

"I'll do it for both of us." He glanced at the rearview mirror. "In fact, we're being followed, and it's not by a Callahan. Aren't you glad you won me now, beautiful?"

Chapter Three

Jace didn't want to scare Sawyer, but she'd been around Rancho Diablo long enough to know the odds against them were long. There wasn't time to coddle her into seeing things his way. He was going to have to give her a push; Sawyer and the babies were his number one priority right now. "How are you for train travel?"

"I'm not," Sawyer said, "going into hiding. I'm not running."

"We are going into hiding. Take your pick. It's either a sunny locale or the mountains. What's your preference?"

"My preference is that you take me home right now. I'll stay in the house my uncle is selling your family, so I'll be close enough for you to keep an eye on."

"This isn't a game," Jace said quietly. "You know that, Sawyer. You know what Wolf is capable of. He means business. I'm not going to risk anything happening to you and the children."

The thought filled him with dread. There was good reason to worry. Taylor, his brother Falcon's wife, had been kidnapped and taken to Montana for months during her pregnancy. Aunt Fiona had been kidnapped, and she'd burned down Wolf's hideout during her rescue. The memory made him smile—but it was also a com-

pelling reason to treat this newest threat seriously. Wolf
had a long memory.

"Okay, here's what we'll do. We're driving to Texas,"
Jace said. "We'll get married, and we'll call our long road
trip a honeymoon."

"You're not going to whitewash us going into hiding
by calling it a honeymoon."

He had one unhappy lady on his hands. But what else
could he do?

In Texas he had family. He couldn't go to Hell's Colony—it was too hot right now with the Wolf situation,
and there was no reason to bring the heat to his Callahan cousins. But they could find a nice, out-of-the-way
cabin deep in the piney woods of East Texas that would
be really hard for Wolf to find.

If Jace had learned anything from the past few years
of being hounded by Wolf, it was that caution was as important as bravery.

His mind made up, Jace sped toward Vegas and, hopefully, a slew of Wedding Elvises eager to say wedding
vows as quickly as possible.

"I ABSOLUTELY AM not going to marry him," Sawyer told
Ashlyn Callahan when they met at the chapel in Vegas.
The place was white, but that was its only concession to
being a wedding stop.

Ash glanced at the pastor and his doughy little wife.
The man had on a tall top hat and wore a white satin suit.
His wife was arrayed in a vintage period gown, purple
with red feathers. "Maybe it wouldn't be my first choice,
either. But it's a good first start."

"First start?" Sawyer stared at Jace's silver-blond-
haired sister. Ash had always seemed like an ethereal

fairy to her—and yet it was said that of all the Callahans, she was the most dangerous. "A marriage only gets started once, doesn't it?"

Ash shrugged. "Where you say the words isn't important. Getting you and my niece and nephew safe is."

A chill swept Sawyer. How did Ash have so much information about her pregnancy, so soon? Callahan gossip always spread like wildfire.

"I just figure it'd be like Jace to split the deck. No commitment." Ash looked at her. "Except to you, it seems."

Sawyer shook her head. "Jace isn't committed to anything except his children. And Rancho Diablo."

"Don't go on what he says, is my advice. My brother never really was much of a talker, not about anything that made much sense." Ash smiled, looking pleased with herself when she realized Jace had caught her jibe. He came over to ruffle her hair.

"Jace, if you mess up my hair, you'll have a scary sister in your wedding photos," she complained. "Your bride thinks you have commitment issues."

He looked at Sawyer and grinned. "I do. But not to the degree that Sawyer does."

She met his gaze. "I'm not marrying you here."

"Well, you have to," Ash said. "At least, you have to try on the magic wedding dress. Fiona sent it with me, said you should try it on. I always think my aunt's advice should be heeded," she said, tugging Sawyer away from Jace's suddenly interested gaze.

Sawyer made herself follow Ash down the hall and into a private room. "I don't want to try on a dress."

"This one you do," Sawyer said. "It's magic."

"That's a myth, a fairy tale." She'd heard about the

dress's supposedly supernatural qualities and didn't believe it. "There's nothing wrong with the dress I have on."

Ash glanced back at her before opening a closet where a long, white bag hung. "If you're going to be a runaway bride, at least do it in style. This dress," she said, pointing to the bag, "exudes style. High fashion, even."

"No, it doesn't," Sawyer said. She wasn't getting near it, wouldn't be enticed to even take a peek. "I saw the dress on Rose when she and Galen were married. It's beautiful and traditional, but not high fashion."

Ash stared at the bag. "I thought a gown that made every woman beautiful would be considered high fashion."

"No. It would be considered lucky."

"Oh," Ash said, recoiling. "We don't do lucky in our family. Mysticism and respect and ancient lore, and perhaps a little supernatural wonder, but never luck."

Sawyer shook her head. "I'm fine wearing what I have on."

"Aren't you afraid you'll regret it?" Ash asked. "You've been rendezvousing with my brother secretly for a long time. You might as well admit you're in love with him. And when a woman's in love, she wants to be beautiful on her wedding day."

Sawyer didn't know what to say to that outrageous statement. Down the hall, a wedding march played— probably for the couple who'd been waiting in the hall nervously when she and Jace had walked into the chapel.

"I'll leave you alone," Ash said. "Give you a chance to collect your thoughts. I won't be far if you want to do some more sisterly bonding. Feel free to call me if you do."

She went out, closing the door behind her. Sawyer

glared at the garment bag. It wasn't going to work. She wasn't going to try on the gown, which was exactly what Ash wanted. Temptation—the Callahans were very good at temptation.

"It may be mission failure," Ash said, coming to stand next to Jace as he waited anxiously for whatever his bride and sister decided. He was well aware that Sawyer would need to be coaxed into marrying him. He'd seen some reluctant brides in his time, but she seemed to take reticence to a new level. He shook his head as his sister patted his back in sympathy.

"It's not mission failure. She wants to marry me." He refused to believe that after all they'd shared, Sawyer didn't want him. She had to know it wasn't just sex for him—and yet he was pretty certain that's what she'd say if he asked her what she thought it was the two of them had going.

He wasn't about to ask how she defined their relationship.

"She probably thinks you were sowing your wild oats, brother," Ash said cheerfully. "After all, you never stepped up to the plate meaningfully."

"Thank you," he said, "I think I had that much figured out. Now if you can wave your magic wand and tell me how to fix it, I'd be happy to listen to that advice."

She fluffed her silvery hair, glancing in a mirror that was hanging in the foyer. "You and I may be doomed to never ease our wild hearts."

He refused to accept that. Sawyer and he had been seeing each other a long time. It had been wild and passionate in the beginning, but then she'd left, and he'd had way too much time to think. To miss her. "What's she doing? Is she ever coming out of that room? Did you make sure there were no open windows?"

Ash looked at him. "I was trying to talk her into trying on the magic wedding dress."

He felt his stomach pitch. "Sawyer won't wear Fiona's magic wedding dress."

Ash gave him a look that said he was crazy, and maybe he was. "Of course Sawyer should be married in the Callahan tradition!"

"I can't believe you dragged that thing all the way here." Struck by a sudden thought, Jace glanced wildly at the door. "You have no idea the trouble it caused our brothers. In almost every single case, that gown tried to wreck everything."

Ash gasped. "Jace! That's not true!"

"It is true." He remembered tales from their brothers with some horror. One bride hadn't seen her one true love—as she'd believed she would, according to Fiona's fairy tale—and had taken off running out the door. That brother had barely been able to get his chosen bride to give the gown a second chance.

Jace had heard other tales, too, and they all made his blood pressure skyrocket with an attack of premonition.

"What about River? The gown saved her in Montana."

"It's a trick, a dice roll. A man doesn't know if the dress is on his side. I don't need that kind of help." Jace looked at the door again, debating knocking on it and demanding that Sawyer come out. She'd been in there far too long. "Are you sure there were no windows in there she could open?"

"There may have been one," Ash said, "but Sawyer isn't the kind of woman who would ditch you in Vegas."

"She ditched me, as you say, for the past several

months." His chest felt very heavy with sadness. "You have no idea what I've been through with that woman. And now you put her in a room with a diabolical magic wedding dress, and I'm supposed to—"

He glared when the door opened. Sawyer came out, wearing the same clothes she had been before. He looked at her, his breath tight.

"Is it time?" she asked.

He hesitated. "Time?"

"To do this thing."

Jace swallowed. "Sure. If you're ready."

"Are you?"

He'd been ready far longer than he'd realized, but he didn't want to seem overeager and scare her off. "Better now than never."

She didn't look certain, and he shrugged, wanting to give her as much space as possible. With the way she clearly felt about getting married, it could do no good to keep pushing her. They said you could lead a horse to water but not make it drink, and Sawyer was as untamed as the black Diablo mustangs in the canyons around Rancho Diablo.

"I am ready," she said. "As long as we agree that we'll revisit this marriage after the babies are born."

"Revisit it? I'm fine with what we're doing." He didn't like the sound of that at all. He'd heard those cold-footed-bride tales from his brothers, too—and a very merry chase some of their women had led them on.

"I'm well aware that your interest in marriage is purely because of the children, and I understand that." She looked at his sister. "Thank you for bringing the dress, Ash. I appreciate the effort you made to get it here, I really do. More than anything, I'm honored that your aunt

Fiona was willing to share a favorite Callahan tradition with me." She looked back at Jace. "But I don't feel like a real Callahan bride, and I don't think I ever will."

No sooner had the words left her mouth than the small waiting area suddenly filled with Callahans and Cashs, all loud and happy, and perplexed to see Sawyer wearing a hot pink dress and not a magic wedding gown. Storm carted in a bridal bouquet for his niece, kissing her before glaring at Jace.

"It's a happy day!" Fiona exclaimed. "The last Callahan bachelor getting hitched!" She beamed with delight. "Come on, dear. Ash and I will help you change."

Jace raised a brow, watching Sawyer sputter her way out of Fiona's clutches. He smiled, seeing his family envelop his bride-to-be with their overwhelming presence. No one irritated him more than his relatives at times, but it was great to have them at his back.

The cake was delivered by two uniformed men who looked a bit seedy to Jace.

"You're putting that there?" Fiona demanded, as they set the cake down in the foyer. "Do we look like we eat wedding cake in doorways?"

They shrugged, and Jace had an uncomfortable feeling he'd seen them before. "Aren't you going to take it out of the box?" he asked.

The men left without saying a word.

"That was odd," Sawyer said.

"Very odd." Ash went to undo the white box. "That bakery came highly recommended, and I'm going to give them a piece of my mind about their delivery service." She peeled the sides of the box down and gasped.

Instead of a plastic bride and groom there was a

butcher knife, splendidly tied with satin ribbon, sticking up out of the top of the beautiful cake.

THE WHOLE THING was a disaster as far as Jace was concerned. Married hurriedly by a satin-wearing pastor who wanted them gone as fast as possible once he saw the butcher knife in the wedding cake—and wed apparently in name only to his pregnant love—Jace found it wasn't a happy-ever-after type of event.

And they'd slept in separate beds after his late-night partying family finally went to bed.

"Very sad state of affairs," he told Sawyer as they drove back toward Rancho Diablo the next day.

She didn't spare him a glance as she looked out the window. "What's a very sad state of affairs?"

"You. Me. That stupid wedding." He gulped, certain that dire consequences might lie in his future. "The whole thing was wrong."

"Wrong?"

"Not traditional." Not done right, not written in stone, the butcher knife notwithstanding.

Traditional was the way he wanted his relationship with Sawyer to be.

"Stop thinking about the cake. It was an accident, like your aunt said. The delivery drivers were new, they didn't know not to put the knife in the same box as the cake, and it somehow got stuck in it. These things happen at weddings."

"I don't think so."

"Anyway, it was delicious. You said so yourself. And the bakery gave Ash a 50 percent discount and told her that if she ever got married, they'd do a cake for her for free."

He wasn't calmed by his bride's attempt to soothe him. Jace was sure he'd seen those delivery guys somewhere, and trying to remember where nagged at him. The bakery had said they'd sent two men to deliver the cake, and the Callahans hadn't thought to ask for ID or names in the shock of the moment. "You could have at least pretended to want to wear the wedding dress Ash went to the trouble to bring you," he groused, thinking he should probably be happy Sawyer had at least said I do. That was something.

Heck, he'd wanted some enthusiasm from his bride. Perhaps even a smile. He was so out of sorts he wasn't even sure why he was complaining.

"I can't feel good about this marriage, Jace. So wearing the dress would be dishonest. I'm too aware that your family doesn't trust me, though they put on a happy face today for you."

So that's what was bugging doll face. He couldn't contradict her, either. The Chacon Callahans as a rule had never really trusted Sawyer's uncle Storm—and Sawyer was assuming that some familial distrust was reflected on her, as well.

"We trusted you enough to hire you, let you bodyguard our children."

"But when Somer and I were at Rose's father's place and fired on each other, and someone conked her father over the head, everything changed. You can't deny that."

He heard the note of sadness in Sawyer's voice. "It was a big misunderstanding. Your cousin and you probably saved Rose that night. Maybe Sheriff Carstairs, too. Hell, even my brother Galen. He's never been a fast runner, though he claims he is, and you and Somer firing at each other gave him the cover he needed to make it inside to Rose."

"I appreciate you trying to make me feel better. But I know in my heart that I was always on a probationary basis with all of you. Only Galen really trusted me. And once I became pregnant…" She glanced at him. "Jace, be honest. It had to have crossed a few of your brothers' minds that maybe I'd become pregnant as part of a plot to get inside Rancho Diablo permanently."

"No one mentioned it." He shrugged. "But you're part of the Callahan family now, and no one's sending up warning flares. In fact, you're the only one who seems bothered by the past. And anyway, we wouldn't have agreed to buy Storm's place if we hadn't decided he was on our side. We don't do business—any kind of business—with folks who are trying to kill us."

She didn't say anything else, conversation over for the moment. He hadn't convinced her that the family accepted her. Only time could solve that problem.

Maybe he could appeal to her feminine side. All the Callahan brides seemed to favor the frilly white fairy tale.

"Look at it this way. Would Ash have taken the time and the trouble to bring you the mystical treasured gown to wear down the aisle if the family didn't consider you one of us?"

Jace wished Sawyer would look at him, but she didn't, nor did she answer. He drove on, wondering if a difficult beginning could ever turn into a happy ending.

Chapter Four

"So the holy grail, as I see it," Jace said to his sister on his cell phone, as Sawyer selected some lunch offerings in a roadside café in New Mexico, "is keeping my bride out of Rancho Diablo."

"That's the family vote. There are a hundred reasons for Sawyer not to be here, and no good ones we can think of for her to be. It's just not safe. She's too good of a bargaining chip. Now that Storm has managed to break any ties Wolf was hoping to bind him with, our uncle will certainly try to get even with hers."

Jace watched his delicate wife as she chatted with the owner of the small mom-and-pop restaurant. Roadside places this size could be greasy spoons, but this one was warm and welcoming. He liked the white paint on the building and the blue shutters that seemed to welcome weary travelers. The full parking lot had been testament to the good eats inside.

"She won't like it," he told his sister.

"We all agree that's the likelihood. We hasten to warn you that Sawyer has left before, when she felt things were not optimum between you. This time, you'll have to figure out how to keep her on the road with you. Unless you can convince her to go into temporary hiding, at least until after the babies are born. We had a family council, and we vote unanimously that less of you is more. Besides, you deserve a honeymoon, brother."

He could hear his sister's giggle loud and clear. "I'll do my best."

"Then that should be good enough. Tell Sawyer hello from the Callahan clan, and congratulations again. There must be a hundred wedding gifts here that she can open when you lovebirds return."

Ash hung up, and Jace went inside to sit in a sunny, cushy booth across from his wife.

"I ordered for you."

"Thanks." He glanced around, checking the other diners. "Ash says the family sends their..." He groped for a word she'd find acceptable.

"Felicitations?"

"Exactly." A waitress put a steaming cup of coffee in front of him, and Jace waited until she was gone. "She says a few wedding gifts have arrived."

"I'll write thank-you letters when we get home."

"Yeah, about that." He rubbed the back of his neck. "Ash also says that we need to stay gone awhile longer."

Sawyer gazed over her glass of tea at him. "Reason?"

He hated to be the bearer of bad news. "Security."

"Your family's afraid I'm on the other side."

"Will you stop?" he demanded impatiently. "They're worried you're a target now that your uncle has crossed Wolf, and therefore the cartel that Wolf is in cahoots with. It's a dangerous situation for all."

Her brow furrowed. "I never thought of that."

"Yeah, well. Neither did I. I'd like to say Ash has worry overload, but considering the knife in the cake—"

"Accidental. Don't let the Callahan love of drama make you see things that weren't there."

His gaze drifted out the window. He saw a truck pass that looked a lot like the one that had been following them on the way to Vegas—and a lightning bolt hit him. The driver of the truck that had been following them had delivered the wedding cake. Maybe Jace couldn't swear to it in a court of law, but there'd been something so familiar about those men.

They'd hijacked the cake and stuck a warning in it.

His neck prickled as he glanced around the diner again, scanning each patron.

"So that's all it is? The reason your family thinks we should stay on the road? Just garden-variety Callahan worry?" Sawyer looked hopeful.

"No," he said quietly. "Ash and my brothers are right. It would be best if we stayed away from the ranch for now."

"If *I* stay away from the ranch," Sawyer said. "You aren't supposed to go back to your home because of me."

"We're together," Jace said. "A team."

"Being married isn't about being guarded, and that's what you're doing."

He shrugged. The waitress laid a piece of apple pie in front of him and a salad in front of Sawyer. She topped off his coffee, then left.

"Salad for you, pie for me?"

Sawyer arched a brow. "I've worked for the Callahans long enough to know what acts like a charm around Rancho Diablo. Nothing brings you running like Fiona's fresh-baked pies and cookies."

This was true. He eyed her salad. "And you don't have a sweet tooth, or are you eating healthy for the babies?"

She waved a fork at his pie. "Just eat, cowboy. I'll take care of myself."

"What would you say," Jace said, looking into her beautiful blue eyes, "to honeymooning in Paris?"

"I would say no, thank you. I'm going back home. A honeymoon isn't necessary." She ate her salad with apparent contentment, which was sort of funny, because he had the calorie-laden, sugar-sprinkled treat, and it tasted like paste to him. It was probably a delicious pie, but he couldn't focus on the tastiness thanks to the woman across from him.

He remembered how good Sawyer's lips felt under his, how amazing it felt to hold her. The pie just wasn't as satisfying.

"I'd take you anywhere in the world you want to go."

"I know." She looked up from her plate. "I get that. I appreciate that you're trying to keep me safe."

"You and my children."

"But you need to be working at Rancho Diablo. You don't need to be babysitting me. I'll be fine." She went back to eating. "Nothing should change because of a wedding ring."

"Everything changed." He drummed the table. "You know that Wolf and the cartel have tunnels running under the land across the canyons? We've bought the property, but there's very little we can do about the underground infrastructure that's already in place. We're pretty certain Wolf intends—or the cartel intends—to try to attack Rancho Diablo from their underground operations center."

"You think they'll eventually tunnel under Rancho Diablo? Why wouldn't they stop at the land across the canyons?"

"Because the goal is to take over the whole ranch." Jace sighed heavily. "Wolf wants the Diablos that live in the canyons. He wants the fabled silver mine, not to mention the ranch itself."

"Is it true about the silver treasure at Rancho Diablo?" she asked curiously.

He started to say, "Hell, yeah, it's true," and stopped himself.

In that moment, he saw the light of curiosity in his wife's eyes die.

But he couldn't tell her the truth.

"I shouldn't have asked," she said quickly. "I'm sorry. I forgot I'm Storm's niece, an outsider, a woman whose uncle once trusted Wolf. Uncle Storm regrets that. He's said a hundred times he wishes he'd never listened to Wolf's lies about your family. But what's done is done."

"Sawyer—"

"It's okay. Really. I'll wait for you in the truck. We need to get on the road if we're going to make it back to Rancho Diablo by nightfall."

She left, and Jace closed his eyes.

She was right on so many levels. And he didn't see any way to change that conflict between them.

Without honesty, a new marriage would have a tough time, especially when it had started as theirs had. Sawyer knew that, too.

He refused to face that ending.

As Jace drove, Sawyer sat quietly, regretting that she'd mentioned the fabled silver treasure supposedly buried somewhere at Rancho Diablo. She'd asked only because the rumor was local lore, but the moment the words were out of her mouth, she'd known she had made a mistake. It was said curiosity killed the cat. In her case, it certainly killed trust. Jace's eyes had darkened and he'd looked away, his mouth tight when she'd asked about the legend—and he hadn't said much since.

She was keeping a secret of her own, a secret that nearly guaranteed an end to their marriage if Jace ever found out. Especially if he was so sensitive about her mentioning a well-known legend in the town of Diablo.

Her uncle Storm had told her to apply at Rancho Diablo, and when she'd gotten the job, he'd asked her to keep an eye out, let him know exactly what was going on with the Callahans. She'd been a sort of double agent, she supposed, working for the Callahans but reporting to Storm, in the beginning.

It wasn't merely idle nosiness, either, not that Jace would understand if she ever admitted her past role. Storm had been approached by Wolf and given a sad story about how his land and mineral rights had been stolen by the Callahans. Storm hadn't known what to think. He'd figured it was none of his business, until he'd caught several scouts trespassing on his ranch, men who worked for Wolf. Wolf had claimed that his "scouts" were doing their job by keeping an eye on land that was rightfully his, which would be borne out by the courts soon enough.

Uncle Storm had done some horse-trading many years back with Jace's aunt Fiona, said matters had gone well enough. He trusted the Chacon Callahans, he'd claimed—except that they didn't trust him, and didn't seem to like him.

Which had made him wonder what they might be hiding. The Chacon Callahans had lived at Rancho Diablo for only the past four years or so. They'd taken over from their cousins, six Callahan boys who'd grown up at Rancho Diablo. Those Callahans had all married, and left in order to keep their families safe—as had their parents.

Her husband's parents, Carlos and Julia Chacon, had gone into hiding, and Running Bear had raised their seven children in the tribe. Jace's Callahan cousins' parents, Jeremiah and Molly, who'd built Rancho Diablo, had also gone into hiding when they'd turned in information about the cartel to federal agents. It had killed Jeremiah and Molly to leave their six boys, their friends, the wonderful Tudor-style home they'd built, Diablo itself. Molly's sister, Fiona, had come from Ireland to raise the six Callahans—as she now tried to take care of the seven Chacon Callahans.

Rancho Diablo was a tempting prize for Wolf, the one son who hadn't fit in, as Jeremiah and Carlos had. Running Bear called Wolf his bad seed, and said sometimes there was no fixing such a black-hearted individual.

There was an awful lot of money at the Callahan place, and the wealth just seemed to grow. Everything the Callahans touched turned to gold—or silver. Times were tough economically for lots of people in the country. How could one family seem to endlessly reap financial rewards, unless maybe they had cut Wolf Chacon out of his portion?

Sawyer's uncle hadn't wanted to get involved, but he'd found himself caught between a rock and a hard place. Between the Chacon Callahans and their uncle Wolf, who'd told Storm his small ranch would be safe if he turned a blind eye to the scouts who roamed his land.

He'd thought to warn the Callahans, had gone over there a few times with wedding or baby gifts, or just to chat, but they'd always seemed to flat out distrust him. He'd been a bit hurt by this, as he'd considered Fiona an honest trading partner. Obviously, times had changed with this new crop of leaner, tougher Callahans.

Yet Uncle Storm didn't trust Wolf, either, and it didn't matter that the man tried to be nice to him. He'd grown uncomfortable, and disliking the neighborly tension, had asked Sawyer to apply for work at Rancho Diablo when her last bodyguard position ended. She had, and to her surprise, was hired.

To her greater surprise, she'd found herself devotedly pursued by Jace. It was said that once you were a Callahan's woman, you were pretty much ruined for all other men, and she believed it. Jace Callahan had completely dashed her desire to even talk to another man, let alone kiss one.

When they were apart, she thought about him constantly.

When they were together, she didn't think at all. She just lived in the moment, in his arms, despite knowing very well that at the end of that silken, sexy road lay unhappiness. No way would a Callahan marry a Cash.

"I think Galen named that land across the canyons Loco Diablo," Jace said, startling her.

She blinked. "Crazy Devil? That's going to be the ranch name?"

"He figured the Callahan cousins own Rancho Diablo, and Dark Diablo in Tempest. So to keep with the naming history, he went with Loco Diablo."

"That's very organized of him."

"Yeah. Ash is roasting him about it. In her mind, she was going to win the ranch."

"Sister Wind Ranch," Sawyer said softly.

He nodded. "But Loco Diablo it is."

"Which is somehow fitting, given that the name was chosen by a Chacon Callahan."

Jace glanced over and caught the smile she hadn't hidden quickly enough.

"You laugh, but you're part of Loco Diablo now. It's where our children will grow up."

She shook her head. "Pretty sure that's not going to happen, Callahan."

"No?" He sneaked a palm over to her tummy, which felt like a pumpkin sitting in her lap. She removed his hand at once. "Where do you figure the children will live, once we get past our Uncle Wolf problem?"

Sawyer wasn't going to let herself consider a future together. "Jace, you know—and everyone knows—that Loco Diablo will never be safe. Even if they blew up the tunnels that are underneath the ranch, even if you somehow managed to run the cartel and your uncle Wolf out of your lives, it still wouldn't be secure. And don't even try to tell me that you've got Wolf on the run. He's never going to give up."

"No argument from me," Jace said cheerfully. "That's why you and I are staying on the road for now. I'm determined to keep you safe."

"I'm the bodyguard," Sawyer said with a touch of heat. "You're the cowboy. I'd be protecting you."

He laughed. "And I'll let you."

Great. He couldn't be serious about anything, least of all how important her independence was, how determined she was to keep maximum separation between them. "This isn't going to work."

"It's going to work, because there are two children counting on us to make it work. We need to choose names for them. That can be our road game until we get to Texas."

"Texas!" She glared at him. "You said you were taking me to Rancho Diablo!"

"Yeah. That was about a hundred miles ago. Now we're driving to Texas, and then on to Virginia. There are some military bases in the Tidewater. But we won't be hanging out in the officers' club or on the strip. We'll be much more undercover than that."

She shook her head. "You can take me straight back to the ranch."

"Babe, listen—"

"Don't 'babe' me. I'm not going anywhere except home. I shouldn't have married you, so don't press your luck."

He sighed, and she gazed out the window again, refusing to bend from her position. "Look, we're married. But that's it. I'll continue to make my own decisions, Jace."

"I expect you to. But eventually, we're going to have to talk about the children and what's best for them."

"So talk." He could talk all he liked, but she wasn't moving to Virginia—or anywhere else—just because he had a nervous streak.

"What about the children?"

She didn't reply, and he continued, "We can't just call them 'the babies.' They need names. I've always liked—"

"I was thinking Jason and Ashley."

"Jason and Ashley?"

"Yes. Jason, obviously, is a variation of your name, and Ashley because I like your sister, Ashlyn."

"I approve. And my sister will be thrilled, I'm sure you know."

Secretly, Sawyer was pleased, though she didn't want to say so.

"I can't believe I'm going to be a father to a little girl and boy. It's so unreal. And wonderful."

It was hard not to soften, hearing the pride in his deep voice. She'd always loved Jace's voice, so warm and enveloping and inviting somehow, especially when he whispered to her in the dark.

She sensed those days were long gone. Nothing could be the same now that they were married, and married under spurious circumstances he'd no doubt come to regret one day. Speaking of regret, she figured she might as well put everything out in the open now. She took a deep breath.

"Jace, here's the main reason you and I have a marriage that's probably going to be in a difficult spot, even if we didn't have a few other notable issues. I know your family really never trusted mine."

"Sort of stating it too harshly," Jace said. "We didn't know what to think. Besides, we've put all that to rest with our marriage."

Sawyer knew better. "In a sense, your family's fears were well-founded. Uncle Storm did ask me to keep an eye on your family."

She turned to look at him, met his surprised gaze. "I'm sorry. I just think you should know the truth."

"We kept an eye on Storm, and will continue to. We keep an eye on everyone. No big deal."

She waved a hand. "You can't brush that off. I was working for you, and reporting to my uncle whenever I saw anything that I thought might be a problem for him."

"Why? We never had anything to do with Storm.

Didn't wish him ill." Jace shrugged. "We just didn't fully trust him."

"Yet you hired me."

"We weren't worried about you."

She didn't know if she should be flattered, or insulted by the sheer arrogance of Jace thinking she wasn't a threat. "Because I'm a woman?"

"No. I wasn't worried about you because—"

"Oh, no," Sawyer interrupted, suddenly annoyed. "You weren't worried about me because you thought you'd locked me down."

He laughed. "I wouldn't have put it that way, but I would say that I feel I'm a pretty good judge of women. You never struck me as a devious sort. I could tell you liked me. Women who are hot for a guy usually have strong loyalty to him."

"Really. Yet I reported on you to Uncle Storm."

Jace shrugged again. "Probably a wise thing to do. Now that you've gotten that off your conscience, should we stop for the night? I don't want you getting too tired. My children need their rest."

She stared at him, not happy at all. "Please drive on. I don't want to spend a night with you." They'd never shared a real bed before; no sense in starting tonight. Her resolve would weaken if she got near her handsome husband and a bed, with no Callahan drama to keep them apart.

"You're having second thoughts? I'm not the date you had in mind when you spent your hard-earned money on me?"

She turned away, glanced out the window. Oh, he was every bit what she'd had in mind, and then some. She was married to the man of her dreams and the father of her children.

What more could a woman ask for from a bachelor raffle?

"You're going to have to help me get Loco Diablo away from Galen," Jace said, "or at least what should be my share of it. Now that you've proved you have a devious streak, that shouldn't be a problem at all, princess."

She turned to face him in disbelief. "You married me to get the ranch?"

He smiled. "We never claimed we were in love, sweetheart."

She was. She had been for a long time. Did he think that she'd risked her job and her reputation to sleep with him just because he was sexy and irresistible? "That's right. It was just a fling. Which proves my point. We have no business being married, but now that we are, I have no intention of letting you use me to oust your siblings from their ranch. You Callahans can work all that out."

"You forget you're a Callahan now."

She hadn't forgotten. But in her heart, she knew her husband still considered her a Cash, even if he didn't admit it.

She'd always be a Cash to him—and likely hers wasn't the family tree he'd ever hoped to graft to his. "I'm a Callahan by name only, according to what you're saying. Everything else is just business."

"It's just business until you decide you want more," Jace said. "As I recall, you're not exactly immune to me. I'm a patient man. I'm willing to wait for you to see the light."

Outraged, Sawyer glared at him. "You're not a patient man. That's why we were married in a quickie Vegas wedding! You couldn't wait to have a reason to throw your name into the hat for the land raffle."

He smiled again. "The fact that I'm going to be a father of twins definitely gives me an edge," he said, teasing, trying to get her goat.

He was succeeding royally.

"This was a terrible idea," Sawyer said. "It's what happens when there's no plan."

He laughed once more. "It's going to work. We have no choice."

Not the tender nothings she'd always hoped to hear on her wedding day. "What a sweet sentiment."

"Kiss me and you'll get more sweetness, babe."

"No, thank you." She wished she could. She'd love to snuggle up against his chest. The problem was that his mouth got in the way, communicating his inner bad boy. Which never failed to rile her.

"After Jason and Ashley are born, you and I are going our separate ways," she said.

"You're not going to help me get my share of the land?"

"I suggest you get a good lawyer for that."

He shrugged. "We have plenty of those."

She looked at him curiously. "Have you ever tried telling Galen that you want a share of the ranch?"

"No. I prefer to do it the honest way. Marriage and babies."

He was impossible. Like all the Callahans, he had a unique thought process. And she was too tired to think through the rabbit trail that was her husband's brain. "I'm going to nap."

"Good idea. I'll still be here when you wake up."

"Lucky me." Sawyer snuggled under the blanket. "Remember—straight back to Rancho Diablo."

She closed her eyes. When she awakened, she'd be that much closer to home.

At last.

Chapter Five

Jace waited for Sawyer to wake up, hoping she'd nap awhile longer. His little wife was sweet, but she had an impressive independent streak, and when she opened her sexy blue eyes and realized they were on the road to a small town in Colorado, there was going to be serious unhappiness happening in his truck.

It wasn't the way he wanted to start his marriage.

Almost as if she sensed his unease, Sawyer opened her eyes, glancing at him. He supposed the hesitant expression on his face probably alerted her that something was going on, because she sat up, looking for a road marker, and found the Welcome to Colorado state sign instead.

She whipped around to glare at him. "What are you doing?"

"It wasn't my idea."

"It sure wasn't mine!"

"No. Running Bear's."

"Running Bear told you we should take a side trip to Colorado?"

Jace nodded. "He called while you were asleep. Asked us to stay away. Just for a few days. Apparently your uncle Storm…" Jace stopped, not wanting to go on.

"What about my uncle?"

"Your uncle is staying at his old place. He moved in there for protection."

"From what? Tell me, Jace. Don't sugarcoat it."

"Nothing exciting," he said. "Just a precaution."

"It's not a precaution," Sawyer said, "if my uncle and his wife have moved back to his old house, a place you now own because he didn't want trouble anymore. The trouble he was trying avoid was between you and Wolf. Why would he go back to where it was happening?"

Jace sighed. "Wolf's put a watch on him, and Lu got a bit spooked. It's nothing to worry about. The sheriff's got men over there, and my brothers and Ash are keeping an eye out. It's going to be fine."

"If it's going to be so fine, why are we in Colorado?"

"Running Bear is operating from an abundance of caution."

"He thinks I'll be kidnapped. It's happened before to Callahan wives."

"You could be used against your uncle," Jace stated, his tone even. "It's not going to happen, because you're my wife, and I'm going to take care of you."

"We've had this conversation," Sawyer said, "and I can take care of myself."

"You'll be housebound soon enough. It's best to take precautions."

Sawyer met his gaze. It was hard to see the distrust in her eyes, so he focused on the road and the directions he'd been given by Running Bear.

"So how long are we operating from an abundance of caution?" Sawyer asked.

"Let's call this our honeymoon. 'Abundance of caution' sounds like unfortunate terminology for newlyweds to use."

She didn't reply.

"So we'll hang out here a day. Then we'll move on to Wyoming."

"Would you care to tell me how long Running Bear advises that we should make ourselves scarce on this honeymoon of yours?"

There was so much tension in her voice. "Not sure," Jace answered. "Hopefully, things will cool down soon." He really didn't know what else to say, though he knew it wasn't a very satisfying answer.

"How long?" Sawyer demanded.

She was already ticked off. Might as well finish off the night with her ticked at him, and then hopefully, the sun would come up tomorrow with all the bad news behind them. "Until after the children are born."

She pulled her phone from her purse. "I'm calling my uncle. I want to check on him and Lu."

"Good idea."

Sawyer barely spared him a glance as she placed the call. "Uncle Storm? It's Sawyer."

Jace finally saw the turnoff that his grandfather had mentioned. He listened with half an ear as he pulled off the main road and followed a smaller, winding road up the mountain. The cabin was well hidden from the trail. Nothing fancy, but secure enough, and not easy to get to unless one had an off-road vehicle. Nobody could sneak up on them here.

He realized Sawyer had hung up. "Any news we can use?"

"Not really," she said.

He couldn't blame her for being unhappy. They were miles from home, and she thought she was stuck with a husband she didn't want.

Only she had wanted him enough to empty her piggy bank for a date. Jace let that cheer him up and give him encouragement that maybe all wasn't over between him and his delicate wife.

"Uncle Storm says he agrees with Running Bear," Sawyer said suddenly.

Jace glanced at her as he parked the truck. "Really?"

She nodded, her blue eyes worried. "I guess that's it, then."

"Look at it this way," he said. "You're getting good value for your money, huh?"

She climbed out of the truck before he could head around to open the door, shutting it with just a bit more force than necessary. He got out, met his bride on the porch of the rustic cabin.

"It's not funny, Jace."

"I wasn't joking, believe it or not. Just trying to put a positive light on things for you." He went around to the back of the cabin, as the chief had instructed, and lifted a board in the floor of the wide back porch. Two wooden chairs and a table gave the place a homey look. He supposed someone had once sat here and stared into the thick woods surrounding the house, maybe gazed at the starlit sky and felt nothing but peace.

He wasn't feeling it yet. Jace stuck his hand under the plank and dug out a key, which was just where the chief had said it would be.

"Whose house is this?"

He patted the board back into place and stood, fitting the key into the lock and turning it. The door opened with a whiney creak, and as he stepped inside he was struck at once by the smell of flowers in the cabin. A vase full of beautiful wildflowers graced the table, welcoming weary strangers. "A friend of the chief's."

Sawyer went into the kitchen. "A good friend. The fridge is stocked."

"Nice." He went to start a fire in the fireplace. There was wood piled up at the back door, so he wouldn't have to gather his own, not for a while.

Depended on how long they were here.

"I'll get you a plate," Sawyer said.

"Thanks." There was central heat and electricity, so this house wasn't completely a rustic hideaway. For that Jace was grateful. He hadn't been sure how much roughing it they might have to do.

"Tea, beer or water? There's even a couple of sodas in here if you're inclined."

"Hot tea sounds fine." Sawyer had to be cold, too. A hot drink would warm them up. He glanced into the kitchen to check on her, suddenly struck by how beautiful she was. Her red hair caught the light from the hanging copper lamps as she filled a kettle with water.

That beautiful woman is my wife.

Holy smokes, I'm actually married.

It was the most amazing realization, and it sent warmth rushing inside him. Pride. Contentment.

He'd be lying if he didn't admit that lust hit him, too. But that part of the marriage was impossible, right?

He'd tell himself a lie: that he'd been driving too long—nearly sixteen hours—and couldn't make love even if Sawyer offered.

Yeah, I could.

He eyed the leather sofa, pretty certain that was going to be his bed for a while. Still, it wasn't his truck, which might be where he slept if he didn't stay out of the doghouse.

"What's wrong?" Sawyer asked, and he glanced up to find her staring at him.

"Nothing." But something was wrong. He had a psychic flare of warning, which didn't make sense, because they were far from danger. He went back to building a fire in the stone fireplace.

"You had the strangest look on your face."

"Probably happens more than I'd like." He held a match under the paper and kindling, and the fire slowly caught.

"Here you go." Sawyer set a red plate on the coffee table. "The tea will be ready in a moment."

He sat dutifully, eyeing the plate. She'd placed a couple slices of cheese, some crackers, a few store-bought cookies and a pile of what looked like delicious chicken salad on it. "That's a feast."

"Somebody was kind enough to save us a trip to the grocery store tonight. Or we ran someone out of their home, and like Goldilocks, we're taking full advantage."

"I don't know. Grandfather doesn't always give the game plan."

"So we're not going to wake up with someone's shotgun aimed at us?"

"I'm not promising that won't happen."

She sighed, picked up a carrot stick. "It's kind of weird that we spent all those months sneaking around, and now we're in a cabin together with a roof over our heads."

And a bed nearby. There's got to be one in this joint. I'd like to have my wife in a bed just once.

Unfortunately, I think those days of Sawyer seducing me are long gone.

It really stinks.

"You've got that funny look on your face again," Sawyer said, "like you're in pain. Isn't the salad good?"

"It's great," he said, as if he cared about anything except Sawyer at the moment, which he didn't. He ate some chicken salad and tried not to think about how much he wanted her, failing miserably.

She gave him a long look, then put her own plate back on the coffee table. "I think I'll try to find some sheets for the beds."

Beds plural. He nodded, sighing inside. What was he, a man of steel? Being on the run with Sawyer was going to drive him mad.

All he wanted to do was take her in his arms and make love to her, the way he had many, many times before, which had been amazing and awesome, and the reason they were here together now as man and wife.

He was shocked a moment later when Sawyer returned and took his hand. He glanced up, meeting her eyes.

"The beds are made. Sheets are fresh. The rooms are really beautiful. I picked one out."

She was beautiful. Why was she holding his hand? "Guess we got lucky."

Sawyer's gaze didn't leave his. She pulled on his hand, and he hesitated—then suddenly got smacked in the face with what was happening.

Maybe.

He didn't dare hope.

Sawyer pulled him down the hall, drawing him into a room that had a large bed with an attractive gold-and-brown comforter on it. A rocking chair and lamp and gold-painted dresser finished the decor.

But he didn't have long to assess the surroundings.

Sawyer looked at him, her eyes big with what seemed like hope and invitation, and he dragged her toward the bed.

It was just like old times, with the heat and the passion and the hot desire running through him.

Yet this time would be different. There was a bed, they were married and he was going to be a father.

It was very different. "Are you sure about this?" he asked.

"I don't do things I'm not sure about."

Jace drew a deep breath. "I'm going to enjoy the hell out of every moment of this."

Sawyer smiled and he took her in his arms.

"Seems odd," she said. "There's a ceiling overhead."

"I know. But you'll still see stars. I promise you that."

Those seemed to be the words needed to trigger the sexy tigress he'd always known Sawyer to be. They pulled each other's clothes off, tossing them to the floor in abandoned piles, and only once did they stop their fevered kissing.

Suddenly, she jerked upright in the bed. "Did you hear something? It sounded like a door swinging shut."

"It was a just a shutter blowing in the wind. It's kicking up out there." Jace was half-naked and his wife's hands had been busily undoing his jeans. He didn't care if Santa was about to scoot down the chimney for a February surprise. Sawyer wanted him, and nothing else mattered.

"I'll go check it out," she said.

"Damn it." Jace got up, zipping his jeans. "You're not the bodyguard in this relationship anymore. You're a mother. You have enough to do. You get naked and be in those sheets when I return. Hell, I don't even care if you're in the sheets. Just be naked when I get back."

The sound had been nothing more than the creak and pop of an unfamiliar house, but his wife's hearing and caution were admirable. Personally, he had so much blood and desire screaming through his head that he'd probably kill any unfortunate intruder that may have crept inside the cabin.

Ash sat in front of the fireplace, warming her hands.

"What the hell are you doing here?" Jace demanded, lust fleeing like a ghost.

His sister shook her head. "I've been assigned to be your lookout. And I'm not happy about it."

"That makes two of us." He sat across from her, and she picked up the plate of food that he'd barely touched.

"Do you mind?" she asked. "I'm starved."

"Have at it." He looked at her. "How'd you get here?"

"I rode a broom," she said, put out with the whole situation. "How do you think? I drove. Grandfather gave me the meet point and here I am. I'd have been here sooner but I had a flat tire in Alamosa." She snacked on the cookies without much enthusiasm. "I always miss Fiona's cooking when I'm away from home."

"You could have gotten here later and that would have been fine," Jace said.

She looked at him, then at Sawyer as she walked into the room wearing his T-shirt and a bathrobe she'd grabbed from somewhere. "Oh. Sorry. Did I interrupt the honeymooning?"

Sawyer smiled. "I don't know if you can really call this honeymooning."

The hell they hadn't been. He'd been about to send his wife into a serious pleasure overdrive, and if that wasn't the definition of honeymoon, he didn't know what was.

Jace went to the fridge and grabbed a beer to mask his grumpiness.

"The chief says he doesn't want any trouble this time," Ash said. "I'm here as an equalizer should any trouble try to rear its head."

"If you've been sent to help, does that mean this is home for a while?" Sawyer asked.

Ash shrugged, crossing her legs underneath her as she finished off her brother's plate of food. "The Feds plan to dynamite the tunnels under Sister Wind Ranch."

"Under Loco Diablo," Jace automatically said, and Ash said, "Whatever. It's going to be my ranch."

"What does Galen think about that?" Jace asked. "His ranch being dynamited?"

"Who cares what Galen thinks?" She smiled at Sawyer. "I don't pay attention to what any of my brothers think if I can help it."

"About the tunnels," Sawyer said. "If they're being dynamited, then that's going to flush out Wolf and his gang, isn't it?"

"That's the problem," Ash replied. "Wolf blames this whole situation on your uncle."

Jace watched his wife's expression turn fearful. "It'll be all right," he said quickly, but Sawyer stared at Ash.

"How could it be my uncle's fault?"

She shrugged. "Wolf let your uncle know that he blames him for the deal falling apart. If Storm had stayed put and not sold his place to us, then Wolf would have continued to have ranch land he could operate from that bordered ours. Now he's out in the open."

"What does that have to do with the tunnels?" Jace asked.

Sawyer looked at him. "Your uncle Wolf thinks I turned on my uncle to marry you."

Jace started to shake his head, then noticed his sister was nodding hers. "I don't exactly get it."

"You'll have to tell him one day," Ash said to Sawyer, who slowly nodded.

"You remember that I told you my uncle wanted me to report to him on anything suspicious your family might be doing, because he wasn't sure who the bad guys and the good guys were?"

"Yeah," Jace said, aware by the pained look on his sister's face that he wasn't going to like what he was about to hear, "but I don't care about that. You're my wife. You're having my children. Everything else is in the past."

"I told my uncle that your family was thinking about leaving the ranch one day," Sawyer said. "Especially since so many of you were married. And since Galen had bought the land across the canyons."

"Sister Wind Ranch," Ash said.

"Loco Diablo," Jace said, trying to figure out why Sawyer was so upset. "I don't see what's wrong. We *will* go home eventually. When the land and the family are safe again, we'll go back where we came from, and our cousins will return to their home."

"I told my uncle that the Callahans could return home any day," Sawyer said miserably. "I didn't mean anything by it. I just wanted to calm him down. He's been so worried for so long. Wolf has really kept him rattled. He started out so friendly, but over time began to change, got more threatening. Uncle Storm panicked, knowing that Wolf's men were close, and realizing that major trouble was coming if your family left Rancho Diablo. As far as my uncle is concerned, your family is strong, and maybe the only people capable of keeping Wolf at bay. So he sold out—to you. Wolf wanted him to sell to him," Sawyer finished. "He's furious with my uncle and promised to take revenge on him the moment his back was turned."

Jace frowned. "This is typical Wolf stuff. If I listened to every threat that came out of Uncle Wolf, I'd be deaf."

"But then the tunnels were reported to the Feds," Ash interjected, "and Wolf believes Storm ratted him out."

"How could he? Storm didn't know about the tunnels."

"He did," Sawyer said with a sigh, "because of me."

Jace felt a dawning sense of dread wash over him. "So? Wolf couldn't know that your uncle knew."

"Wolf knew," Ash said, "because your wife was wired up."

Jace stared at his wife, stunned. "Wired?"

"I thought I'd been wired by the Feds," Sawyer said miserably. "But it was Wolf's men, trying to get intel on your family."

Her pretty blue eyes welled with tears, and Jace's world turned on its head. "You ended up giving information to the enemy about your own uncle?"

"And you," Sawyer said. "About the Callahans."

"It's not possible that you're a double agent!" Jace felt his heart stop in his chest. "You were sleeping with me every chance we got."

She blushed, and he felt a twinge for embarrassing her in front of Ash. But her betrayal had sent the words rocketing out of his mouth.

"Again, I thought I'd been wired by the Feds. They told me it was to protect your family, in case another one of the Callahans was kidnapped. They said Ash was wearing a wire, too."

"You didn't ask my sister if any Feds had questioned her about the tunnels? Or wired her?" Jace demanded.

"Actually," Ash said, "I was wired. But I knew it was a trick, and I just played along to find out what I could about Wolf's operations."

"Have you lost your mind?" Jace demanded of his sister. "Do you realize the danger you put yourself in? What if Wolf had snatched you?" Anger rose inside him as he stared at the two most important women in his life. "Go outside," he said to his sister. "I have to talk to my wife."

Ash got up, slipped on her coat and went out the door. He heard a rocker scrape as she pulled a chair to the rail so she could stare into the forest. He glared at Sawyer, who tugged the blue robe around her more tightly. "I don't think I completely understand why you did what you did. But what I do understand is that you're not quite the bodyguard our family thought you were."

"Jace—"

He held up a hand. "You've endangered yourself, you've endangered my children, your uncle, my family." Jace stared at her. "I can't trust you."

"Were you ever going to trust a Cash?" she asked, her tone bitter.

Jace looked at her, wondering if the overwhelming pull he'd always felt for Sawyer had somehow clouded his mind, kept him from seeing her for what she really was. Maybe it had. He'd missed her like hell when she'd left Rancho Diablo. When she'd returned, he'd been relieved, and most of all, felt alive again.

"I don't know," he finally said. "Maybe I was too blind to see it." Perhaps what he loved most about Sawyer was that she was life on the edge, the walk on the wild side that brought amazing emotions rushing through him.

"Maybe trusting you was my Achilles' heel. A weakness I brought on my own family."

He left the kitchen and went to sit outside on the front porch, away from his sister, and definitely as far away from his wife as he could get. The moon hung full overhead, and the sky promised cold, and no doubt snow by morning. A tinge of fear gripped him, and his grandfather's warning crept into his mind: one of the Chacon Callahans was the hunted one, the one who would bring danger and darkness to the family. Jace had always been so certain it wasn't him. He felt his roots deeply, both in the tribe and in his Callahan lineage.

But he had brought danger to the family by marrying Sawyer. He'd married her, for God's sake.

There'd been no choice. Not just because of the children, but because he loved her. He wouldn't admit that to a single soul, but he was in love with a woman who seemed to have different faces, different lives.

The lightning-strike tattoo on his shoulder, which all the Callahan siblings had—the sign of their bond—burned suddenly, as if he was being branded.

Jace looked up at the full moon above and wished like hell he hadn't found out who his wife really was.

He'd been sleeping with the enemy. For many long, tortured nights, he'd known his soul was hers.

He'd brought the enemy to Rancho Diablo. And made her a Callahan.

Chapter Six

"She's gone," Ash said, when he walked back inside the small cabin the next morning. His sister looked nonplussed as she snacked on some cookies and a cup of coffee.

"She isn't gone." Jace tossed his coat into a chair. He'd spent an uncomfortable night on the front porch, unaware of the time passing as he watched the snow drift down. It had piled up, maybe three inches, while he'd sat and stared at it. He'd felt dead inside, immune to cold and fear.

All he could do was play over and over in his mind how Sawyer could have betrayed him—and how he could have been too blind to recognize it. "Sawyer couldn't have left. I was sitting out front the entire night. Anyway, she's my wife. Right now, she needs me. She's pregnant with twins."

"I know." His sister brought him a mug of black coffee. "You forget she's a very well-trained bodyguard. Perhaps you even forget how skilled she is at not just protection, but evasion. It's why Kendall felt secure hiring her for the twins. Don't you remember this?"

"She must still be here, Ash. There's no place for her to go."

They were halfway up the mountain, maybe more.

The road down would be a challenge, even if she'd stolen his truck.

"She took my Jeep," Ash said.

He stared at his sister, reality socking him in the face. "How in the hell did that happen?"

Ash shrugged. "I gave her my keys."

His jaw dropped. "What?"

"She wanted to go. I gave her my keys, told her how to get off the mountain without driving past your snowbound lair out there."

"You had my pregnant wife drive up to the top of this mountain and go down the other side, in this weather, without even knowing if the roads were passable at the top?" He slumped into a chair at the table, unable to look away from Ash's gamine face. She stared at him calmly.

"You can't keep her prisoner."

"I know that! She wasn't a prisoner, damn it. We had things to work out." She'd kissed him just as passionately as he'd kissed her last night, and he'd been pretty certain they were about to finally find out what making love together in a bed would be like.

And now this bombshell.

He felt wrecked.

"I'm so sorry, brother," Ash said. "I usually don't get involved in people's personal lives."

"You always get involved in everybody's personal lives," Jace said.

"What I mean is that I would never have done it, except that I can't bear for anything to be trapped. You know that." Ash stared at him. "Sawyer seemed as lost as the animals I do rescue work with. I wanted her spirit to be as free as the Diablos. You know how important that is."

He grunted, not happy.

Ash put a hand on his arm as she sat next to him. "Brother, it's bad to start off a marriage with one person feeling trapped. That's not the way you want Sawyer."

He just wanted her. He didn't really care how he got her.

Which was a problem.

"She'll come to you," Ash said.

"Runaway brides usually run for a reason."

His sister sighed. "Okay, I don't know that she'll come back for sure. But you two have a lot to build on."

"Not really."

"The children, Jace. They'll be a huge part of your lives."

He nodded. "Sharing custody with my wife isn't what I had in mind." No doubt Sawyer would want to divorce him now. Maybe even annul the marriage. Damn it, she might ask for a divorce *and* an annulment, which would stink to high heaven.

"She's just heartbroken," Ash said.

"Sawyer is heartbroken?" He got up and moved to stare out at the dawning sky.

"She knows you don't trust her."

"That's a whole other problem."

"Jace, relationships are built on mutual trust and respect."

He shook his head. "There's no reason for us to stay here. Come on. Pack your bags."

"Bags? Since when do I travel with a bag?" His sister stood, reached for her coat and backpack.

"Whose joint is this, anyway?" He glanced around one final time. It was a great place for a honeymoon—if two people wanted to be alone together. Sawyer hadn't wanted that.

"It's Grandfather's," Ash said, sounding surprised.

Jace took further stock of the cabin. "It can't be. It's too frilly."

She smiled. "Poor Grandfather. Don't you think he has a life of his own?"

Jace looked at her. "What are you trying to tell me?"

"Close your eyes."

His sister was trying his patience, but he complied.

"What do you feel?" she asked softly.

"Pissed."

"Besides that. Look beyond your own emotions."

He focused on the smell of the cabin, the feel of the hot mug in his hand, the sense of home that pervaded every corner of the small house. "A woman lives here. A happy, contented woman." He opened his eyes.

Ash smiled at him. "Yes, she does."

"Who?"

"You're older than me. You have to remember more." She slung her backpack over her shoulder. "It's time to go."

He followed his sister out, glanced behind him one last time, then locked the door. After putting the key back under the board where he had found it, he stared at the cabin a moment longer, its presence in the wooded mountain joyfully framed by the sun. Icicles hung from the eaves, and in the sky overhead, a hawk soared.

He looked at Ash. "Our parents?"

She smiled. "I don't know where our parents are. I only know I feel their spirits here."

Jace followed her to the truck and they got in. "Grandfather told you something."

"He told me that the cabin is the family's. That it's vacant right now because it always is in winter. Winter can be harsh on the mountain."

Jace drove slowly through the snow. "It's not the winter that's harsh here. It's the loneliness and solitude."

"That's right."

He was amazed by his sister's knowledge. She always seemed sort of otherworldly—had from the time she was born. "Did you even try to talk Sawyer into staying?" He'd liked to have told Sawyer about his parents. They'd never mentioned their families to each other. He had a faint memory of his mother and father; as the second eldest, he'd been old enough to remember when they'd gone.

It had been like a knife wound in his heart that hadn't eased for years. For so long he'd felt deserted, betrayed, angry. He'd known why they had to leave, but he was still angry at the people who'd made them go.

The same people for whom Sawyer had been wearing a wire. Betrayal and anger ripped through him again. "How could Sawyer do it?"

"Family is important to her."

"Damn it, I'm supposed to be her family. We've made a family together!"

"Easy, hoss," Ash said. "No one ever said our lives were going to be easy. The path isn't straight, with magical road maps."

"I know that." He knew that only too well.

"We are all on the journey, even Sawyer."

He grunted. "You're starting to sound more like Running Bear all the time."

"I hope so," she said softly, so softly that he glanced at her curiously.

"What's wrong?"

"Nothing," Ash said. "It's just that sometimes I know I'm not as good as Sawyer is. Or even my brothers. I'm the misfit in this family."

"Ash!" Jace was completely stunned by her words. "You're not a misfit at all!"

"I'm going to sleep," she said, sticking her backpack under her head for a pillow. "Wake me when we cross the state line."

"Why the state line?"

"Because it's important to see where I've been and where I'm going."

Jace was bothered by her words, but not really certain why. He should be angry with her, yet he wasn't. In a way, she'd helped him and Sawyer. Ash was right: Sawyer's confession had changed everything. They needed time to absorb the new twists in their relationship. He still couldn't believe Sawyer had meant to harm his family. She'd won him at the ball for a reason, and it hadn't been just to tell him about the babies.

Ash was right: the path didn't point straight, with a magical road map. In fact, it was bumpy as hell and strewn with potholes.

He'd see his wife soon enough, and then they'd get everything worked out. Somehow.

"It's not going to work." Sawyer laid Ash's keys on the kitchen counter and looked at Fiona Callahan, the eccentric aunt of the Callahan clan. "Jace doesn't trust me. And he has no reason to." She took a deep breath. "Fiona, I need a place to stay, but it can't be here. Nor at my uncle's old place." She'd be too close to Jace, and she knew

Running Bear wouldn't want her staying anywhere near Rancho Diablo, anyway.

Fiona shook her head. "You just let me pour you a cup of tea, Sawyer. You look exhausted. It's a long drive from Colorado. Goodness, you should have flown!"

"I wanted to drive. I like driving to clear my thoughts."

"Well," Fiona said, putting a pretty china cup with pink flowers on it in front of her and a bowl of sugar cubes next to that, "Jace is going to want you to be with him, so you might as well get used to the idea. I'd stay put until he gets back."

Sawyer picked up the delicate cup. "Fiona, I can't. You don't understand what I've done. He has a reason to feel the way he does."

"Let's let Jace decide how he feels, shall we?" The older woman slid a piece of spice cake next to Sawyer's tea. "Patience rules the day, I always say."

Patience wasn't going to help her. Sawyer was so ashamed she could hardly bear it. Everything had happened so quickly, had gotten away from her. She'd prided herself on being a competent bodyguard, and then had let herself operate from a position of weakness. Let herself be wrangled into a bad situation that could never be fixed.

"Why don't you go upstairs and take a little nap?" Fiona suggested.

"Why are *you* still here?" Sawyer asked suddenly. "If it's so dangerous at the ranch, with the Feds and the spies and the reporters crawling everywhere, why haven't your nephews made you leave?"

Fiona smiled. "When you're my age, you get to do as you please. And I cook." She tried to sound light-hearted, saw that Sawyer wasn't convinced. "I've already been kidnapped by Wolf, and he doesn't want me again.

Have you forgotten I burned his last haunt down to the ground?" She looked very satisfied by that. "Life is good in my world."

"I can't wait to be at that point."

"You're closer than you think." Fiona smiled at her, then turned to put a sheet cake in the oven. "It's all about believing in your purpose."

"Maybe." Sawyer's purpose had changed. Maybe that was the problem: she'd drifted. Gotten off course.

"Wait until those babies are born. You'll have so much purpose you'll be overflowing with it. Everything will get better."

Not if her marriage wasn't going to work out. "I betrayed your family, Fiona."

"Let us decide that. Even if you did, what really happened? Isn't our house still standing? Aren't we still a family?" Fiona topped off her tea. "No one can take the important things in life away, if one knows what those treasures are."

"You're trying to make me feel better."

"And I'm succeeding. Now eat that cake. I made blue-ribbon spice cake, my dear, and there's nothing better in February than homemade spice cake with cream cheese frosting."

Sawyer dutifully ate a bite—and to her surprise, the cake actually seemed to make her feel better. Or maybe it was Fiona, or being in the house where Jace lived. Hope rose inside her.

Maybe things could work out, after all. Maybe he wouldn't regret marrying a woman from the wrong ranch.

Maybe he would.

Chapter Seven

Sawyer was in bed upstairs at Rancho Diablo, as Fiona had talked her into staying at least for the night, when she heard the measured tread of boots outside her door. She raised up, waiting to see if the man standing outside her door would knock. Her heart beat faster, waiting—then crashed a little when the footsteps went down the hall.

She lay back down to stare at the ceiling. No matter what Fiona said, the marriage was over before it had even started. Suddenly, the room felt too warm. Her conscience weighed on her terribly, and the regrets seemed overwhelming. The babies kicked inside her, unsettled by her restlessness.

She was in a beautiful home with wonderful people whose trust she wanted more than anything, a family she desperately wanted to be part of. The seven-chimneyed Tudor house with the expansive grounds had always seemed like heaven to her, but the Callahans were the heart and soul of Rancho Diablo. There wasn't one she didn't like, and they'd treated her so well. They were the family she'd never really had—except for Uncle Storm.

She'd never be part of this family now. She'd always be an interloper.

The thing was, she'd do it all over again if it meant giving Uncle Storm the help he needed. She was no different from the Callahans, who were determined to protect their family from Wolf and his gang of dangerous cutthroats.

She sighed, trying to get comfortable, and put a hand over her swiftly growing stomach. It still felt so strange to think of Jace as her husband. She'd known eventually her house of cards was going to fall in on her—but she'd wanted him so much. Saying no had never been an option, and she didn't regret one single moment of their adventuresome lovemaking, either.

Sawyer jumped when someone knocked briskly on the door, then eased it open.

"Sawyer."

She sat up. "What?"

"I'm coming in."

Just like a Callahan, to announce and not ask. "Fine." She sat up, flipped on her bedside lamp. Her eyes went wide as she stared at the handsome man whom she'd deserted not that many hours ago. "You look terrible."

"Thanks." Closing the door, Jace sat on the foot of her bed, frowning, royally displeased.

She couldn't blame him.

"What happened?" Sawyer ran her gaze over Jace's hands, which bore a few cuts that hadn't been there last night. His dark hair was a bit wilder than usual, and his face looked drawn.

"Nothing."

"Nothing you want to talk about, you mean. Quite clearly, something happened."

He shook his head. "Long drive home."

She'd made the same drive, so that wasn't a good excuse. "Let me get you some bandages and some ointment."

"I'm fine," he snapped. "I don't need any coddling."

"Okay," she said, just as snippily, and shrugged. "Suit yourself." All she needed was a grumpy cowboy with his dark side in a twist to put the final icing on her day. It was plain he was angry, and she couldn't blame him.

But if he wanted to sit there like a big miserable lump, she was going to go to sleep. There was no point in talking to him if all he was going to do was glower at her.

"Here," Jace said, pulling a tiny white box from his sheepskin jacket and handing it to her.

"What is it?"

"The purpose of a box is to make the person receiving it open the damn thing," he said crossly.

"I don't want to." She was dying to. But she didn't want gifts. She wanted to start over, with forgiveness as the beginning point.

And lots of hot, sexy kisses.

"Then don't. It's clear no one's going to make you do anything you don't want to do."

She put the small box on the nightstand and glared at her husband. "I had to leave, and you know it as well as I do. There's no point in rehashing what I told you in Colorado, and I wish I hadn't done what I did, but I don't really know how I would have done anything differently." She took a deep breath. "Also, there's no need for you to feel like you have to protect me. I'll get my own bodyguard, Jace. What I want is…"

She stopped, and he looked at her curiously. "What?"

"Something I can't have," she finished miserably. "I don't want presents, either. I never meant for you to have to marry me, and I should have dug my heels in on that. Especially since I knew I was hiding a secret."

He nodded. "Very dishonorable of you, that secret-keeping business."

"Probably," she said hotly, "but you Callahans bring a lot of misery on yourselves. You were never nice to my uncle. What was I supposed to do?"

"I don't know," he said, sounding tired. She gazed at her big, strong husband, noting the heaviness in his eyes. He looked so sad that she ached. "I probably would have done the same thing," he said, his gaze drifting down to the Under Construction message on her T-shirt, stopping at her watermelon-shaped belly. "How do you feel?"

"I feel fine. Although I'll admit the babies are keeping me awake tonight. They're doing gymnastics."

It wasn't the babies keeping her awake, of course. It was the sexy cowboy sitting on her bed.

"That's good. They'll be big and strong." That pronouncement wiped a bit of the annoyance from his face, and Sawyer thought Jace looked plenty pleased with himself now. "Let me know if you need anything." He got up and went to the door, before turning back to face her. "It wasn't my intention to make you feel trapped."

"I know. I just spooked. And I wish our situation could have started out better." Sawyer shook her head. "I think I probably make you feel trapped."

He shrugged. "I shouldn't have taken you to Las Vegas. Or Colorado."

Was he saying he was sorry he'd married her? Icy worry flooded her. That was the last thing she wanted. "I'm glad we got married. You were right about that. For the children."

"Yeah, well, they'll have plenty of documentation. Ash has put about fifty photos of the ceremony on the website."

"Website?" Sawyer hadn't known Rancho Diablo had one.

He nodded. "Running Bear's brainstorm."

She started to ask when his grandfather had become interested in having a site for the ranch, but then realized there was no point in making Jace feel she was digging for information. "That was nice of Ash to commemorate the ceremony. Although we weren't there long enough for fifty photos. And I didn't see her with a camera that much." Sawyer had been too busy ogling Jace.

"You'd be surprised what my sister can do."

"I am sorry about everything, Jace," Sawyer said, meaning it.

"I am, too. And as much as I know this is going to be like throwing kerosene on a fire, you're going to have to leave here tomorrow."

He was right, but it felt as if a fire exploded in her heart at the thought that he was anxious for her to leave. "I know. I told Fiona I needed to go somewhere."

"Aunt Fiona says you should stay, but the situation isn't stable."

"You don't have to explain."

He leaned against the wall. "I'm not explaining. I'm just telling you what's the safest thing for the children. And you."

Silence stretched between them for a long moment. Sawyer looked away, knowing that the days of their stolen meetings were gone forever now.

She missed that so much, missed the wild side of him, and her, and holding him in her arms.

"Jace, I want you to know that I always, always took the very best care of the Callahan children. I guarded them, and would protect them still, with my life. I adored those kids, and would have never allowed anything to happen to them."

He studied her, and she thought she saw anger and betrayal flash in his eyes. "We'll see," Jace said. "We'll see."

Then he left.

ASH KNOCKED NOT thirty minutes later, whispering "Sawyer!" through the door.

"Come in, Ash." Sawyer sat up and turned the bedside lamp on again as Jace's sister slipped inside and made herself at home on the foot of the bed.

"You're not asleep," Ash observed.

"No, I'm not." She hadn't been able to sleep after Jace came to her room. Her thoughts churned restlessly. "Neither are you."

"I don't sleep much."

Ash looked perky, too pleased to be awake at nearly midnight, Sawyer thought crossly.

"Let's sneak downstairs and get a midnight snack," Ash suggested.

"Sure, why not?" Lying in this bed wasn't going to do her any good, anyway. "I assume you have something on your mind, and I might as well hear it with a brownie and some milk."

"It's sheet cake today," Ash said. She got off the bed and bounded over to the nightstand as Sawyer dressed in maternity jeans and clogs and an oversize thermal T-shirt. "What's this?" She held up the white box Jace had given her.

"I didn't open it." And she wasn't going to.

"Is it from Jace?" Ash looked at her. "Yes, I know I'm

snooping, but most people can't leave a box unopened without peeking. At least I can't."

Sawyer smiled, her crankiness chased off a little by Ash's enthusiasm. "I usually can't, either. And yes, it's from your brother."

"Your husband," Ash said. "A wife should immediately open something from her husband."

Sawyer blinked. "I don't want gifts from Jace."

"Oh, pooh. Knowing my brother, it's likely those trick snakes that come flying out. Or something else equally unromantic." She sighed dramatically. "I don't know where we went wrong with him."

Sawyer looked at the box, which Ash was gently shaking next to her ear. "If you're curious, you're welcome to open it."

"I'm curious as a cat! But I never open anything that doesn't have my name on it. It's bad juju."

Sawyer laughed. "You'd open anything, most especially if it didn't have your name on it."

"Okay, that may be true. But not this box. It sounds like jewelry."

"How does jewelry sound?" Sawyer was a little shaken. She didn't want jewelry from Jace. She wanted *him.* She wanted his babies.

Most of all, she wanted his trust—and love.

"It sounds romantic," Ash said, teasing.

"Oh, for heaven's sake. It's not jewelry. When did Jace have time to shop for that? You two were on the road all day, just like I was."

"Yeah, and I got my ear gnawed off by my brother for giving you my keys." Ash looked unfazed and maybe a bit cheerful about her part in Sawyer's escape. "He was grumpier than a hungry baby all the way home."

"Sorry about that."

"Not at all," she said. "Come on, let's go hit Fiona's treasure trove of goodies. My sweet tooth is in withdrawal."

Sawyer looked at the box Ash had put back on the nightstand and seemingly forgotten. She glanced at Jace's sister, who was laughing at her.

"You might as well open it," Ash said. "Now that I've made you think about it, it's going to stay on your mind."

Sawyer tried to act as if she wasn't dying of curiosity as she picked up the box and tore off the white wrapping paper. She made short work of opening the lid, and pulled out a white jeweler's case.

"It might be jewelry," she admitted, and Ash laughed.

"It might be."

Sawyer gave her sister-in-law a curious look. "Do you know what it is?"

"I promise you I do not. He didn't stop at a store while we were on the road."

Sawyer opened the case, then gasped at the engagement ring inside. A large emerald-shaped diamond stared up at her, set in a white-gold setting, or maybe platinum. Tiny baguettes glittered on each side, catching the light like perfectly shaped pieces of ice. "It's gorgeous."

"Wow," Ash said, coming to inspect it. "I didn't know Jace had it in him."

Sawyer felt her hands shaking. All she could do was stare at the stunning ring.

"Well, try it on!" Ash prompted.

"I— Oh, all right." She was dying to. Slipping it on her finger, she was amazed that it fit, and amazed how much she didn't want to take it off.

"Dang," Ash said, "my brother's a romantic, after all."

Sawyer removed the ring and put it back in the box, which she set on her nightstand.

"What are you doing?" Ash demanded.

"I'm going to go get some of Fiona's sheet cake and milk. What you are doing?"

"What about the ring?"

"It stays in the box," Sawyer said, opening her door, "until I talk to your brother and find out exactly what this marriage is all about."

"Noble of you, but I'm too hungry to admire your nobleness. I spent many hours on the road getting my ear chewed off. Let's go do girl talk over sheet cake. We have things to discuss, if you can tear your mind off my brother for thirty minutes," Ash teased.

Sawyer's breath was still stolen by the lovely gift from Jace. She followed Ash into the hall, but couldn't help glancing toward Jace's closed door. Her cowboy had another think coming if he thought he could romance her with diamonds. He could—and it would be hard to hold out against that—but she was after the ultimate prize.

His heart.

JACE SAT UP when he heard his bedroom door creak open. He glanced at the military watch on his arm. Two in the morning. "Who is it?"

"Sawyer."

He felt the side of his bed sink a bit as his wife sat down next to him. He wished he could see her, but was afraid if he turned on the light, she wouldn't say whatever it was she'd come to say. "What's on your mind?"

"So much is on my mind."

He heard the hesitation in her voice. "It's understandable. A lot has happened fast."

"Yes."

He wanted everything to happen faster; he wanted her faster than it seemed he could ever get her.

So he did the only thing he could do—he scooped his wife into the bed with him. Too surprised to move, Sawyer lay still, and he wrapped his arms tightly around her.

"Ahh." Jace sighed with heartfelt satisfaction. "So this is what it feels like to hold you in a real bed."

Chapter Eight

Sawyer was so stunned when Jace pulled her against him that it never occurred to her to move away from her husband or get out of the bed. It felt amazing to be back in Jace's arms again, and she wanted to lie with him like this forever. She was afraid if she left now, she would never get the courage to come back. It had taken every ounce of courage she had to slip into his room, with the full intention of telling him she couldn't accept his beautiful ring.

But that thought flew from her mind the moment Jace reached for her.

She wanted him to kiss her, make love to her.

"Babe?"

"Yes?"

"Are you okay with this?"

Sawyer closed her eyes in the darkness. "I am if you are." The guilt she'd been holding inside weighed on her, but being with him like this made her believe that maybe they could move past everything.

He rolled her toward him, gently pressed a kiss against her lips. She froze, waiting to see what he'd do next, then thought *I'm not waiting any longer* and kissed him back. Their kisses turned urgent and Sawyer felt consumed by Jace in the best kind of way. He ran a hand along her back, cupper her bottom and groaned, the way she'd heard him groan many times before.

It thrilled her, and she didn't want him to stop.

"You feel amazing," he said. "I've missed holding you." He put a hand on her stomach, tracing the fullness there. "I don't want to do anything to hurt you."

Sawyer kissed him. "You're not going to hurt me."

He pulled off her top, tossed her pants to the floor. Just like the old days—almost—he was quick to get rid of her clothes, and she dispensed with his, her hands racing to hold him.

"Wait," Jace said. "I've finally got you in a bed. I'm not rushing this." He pushed her back on the pillows, kissed his way to her breasts, teased her nipples before pressing kisses against her tummy. "I've waited so long for you," he said, parting her legs, "to be in a bed, where I can take my time, without wondering if someone's going to see us in the great outdoors."

She squeezed her eyes closed, her heart beating crazily as he stroked the inside of her thighs. He kissed her most private place, his tongue searching, and Sawyer cried out as she went over the edge into pleasure, unimaginable pleasure.

"Come here," Jace said, pulling her on top of him so that she could straddle him. "You set the pace."

She sank onto him, her body accepting him easily—gladly.

"Oh, God," Jace said with a groan, "I've missed you. I've missed *this*."

He held her close, and she sensed him trying hard not to grind his hips against her the way he wanted to.

"You're not going to hurt me," Sawyer told him.

"I'm not going to find out. We have years to get wild. Tonight, gentle is the key."

He tensed when she ground down upon him, anyway. She took pleasure in tormenting him just a bit, easing up and moving slowly while holding his eyes with hers.

"You tease," he said.

"Yes, I do."

He kissed her, holding her close. Suddenly Sawyer felt pleasure sweeping her, rising inside, eager to push her into love's mystery. She tightened up on Jace, kissing him harder, taking him with her as she began to move faster.

When the pleasure hit them, it was as if a tidal wave that had been cresting forever finally broke, leaving them helpless in each other's arms.

"Don't leave again," Jace said, ten minutes later, when she lay in his embrace, stroking his hair. "Whatever we have to do, we can work it out."

Sawyer swallowed hard as she sprawled on his chest. There was nothing she wanted more—and yet he knew as well as she did that sleeping with her had brought trouble right to his door.

She wasn't sure how to change that, either.

"TELL ME WHAT happened to your hands," Sawyer said in the night, when Jace turned her over to make love to her again.

He hesitated in the darkness, ran a rough palm gently over her breasts. "I removed someone from the premises before I came upstairs. It was no big deal."

She froze. "You got in a fight?"

"It wasn't just me. Dante, Tighe and I found someone on the grounds who didn't want to leave as quickly as we wanted them to."

Chills ran over her. "Did they hurt you?"

"Do I seem like I'm hurting?" He pushed her legs apart with his knee and kissed her. "It was no big deal."

Her breath caught when he entered her.

"Tell me if—"

"You're fine. Quit worrying." Sawyer gasped. She gave herself up to her husband, knowing he wasn't telling her everything, was holding something back.

Yet she'd kept things from him, too.

Maybe it didn't matter. She clutched his shoulders, wrapped her legs around him as he steadily, gently stroked inside her, filling her with everything she'd been missing for too long. Sawyer closed her eyes, felt passion igniting between them, and started falling into the pleasure waiting for her.

The truth was, she'd do anything to keep Jace. She'd "bought" him at auction, and she'd married him despite knowing she had a secret she should have admitted up front.

Maybe she was a terrible person—but she had her cowboy.

She surrendered, drowning in the sexy pleasure, loving the feel of Jace finding his own release inside her.

I never really thought I'd have him. I'll do whatever is necessary to keep him, she thought as he cradled her in his strong arms. Was it wrong to want him so much?

She lay against his neck, feeling his heartbeat and his slow relaxation into sleep.

I'll ask him tomorrow, she thought. *I'll ask him who they tossed off Rancho Diablo. No more holding back between us.*

Sawyer fell asleep with Jace's hand on her stomach, warming her, holding his children.

Holding her heart.

JACE RODE HARD toward the canyons, away from Rancho Diablo and the temptress who was still asleep in his bed. He'd wanted desperately to crawl back in and make love to her again, but at 4:00 a.m. and with chores to be done, sanity had returned.

He had a tiny problem. His wife had spied on his family, and he was going to have to explain the situation to them, in words his ham-headed brothers could understand.

"What are you going to do?" Ash asked as they pulled up near the canyons.

"What can I do? She's my wife. She's having our children." *And I'm in love with her.*

I certainly didn't make my downfall too hard on her.

"You have to forgive her for the sake of the babies," Ash said practically.

"I have forgiven her, damn it." Jace put binoculars up to his eyes, checking the activity on Galen's newly acquired land. It looked as if the Feds and reporters and various authorities were determined to turn the land inside out. In the end, it wouldn't come to anything. By now, Wolf had moved anything of strategic value out of the tunnels, relocating his operations the devil only knew where. "I'm just watching my back so a knife doesn't land in it."

He felt Ash's glance on him before she looked through her own binoculars. "I guess I can't blame you for feeling that way."

"I wouldn't care if you did blame me. It's the way I feel. I stepped in the trap, and I'll decide how it affects me. I know that Sawyer probably gave up some strategic information without meaning to. She thought she was protecting her uncle. I'm okay with that." Jace understood that family was all that mattered.

"You can't be a jerk to your wife, though. It'll be bad for her pregnancy, bad for the children. Bad for both of you."

"Thanks, Madame Buttinski, but I think I've got it handled."

"Jerk," Ash said. "I like Sawyer. I want both of you to be happy."

"I like Sawyer, too." Too damn much. Making love to her in a real bed, taking his sweet time with her, had nearly annihilated any good sense he had. "Don't worry. I've got this. Sawyer and Storm are playing on our team now." Jace was certain of that.

"Of course they are," his sister said impatiently, "now that you're married. The ties that bind and all that. Before, she had little choice. But you're her family, we're her family, and I think she needs to tell the family that Rancho Diablo comes first in her heart now."

"Confession?" He put the binoculars away. "Maybe. I'll cross that bridge when I come to it." It occurred to him that Sawyer wouldn't want to make a confession to the family. Least said, soonest mended. On the other hand, they really didn't know everything she'd revealed, and maybe Ash was right. It might be best if they cleared the air. "Shall we ride over to Galen's kingdom?"

"It bugs you that he bought the land, doesn't it?" she asked curiously.

"It bugs me as much as it bugs you."

"True," Ash agreed, "but I'm not married with kids. You are. So you actually would have been up for the new ranch."

He glanced at his sister. "I'm guessing you haven't heard from Xav Phillips lately."

Her face pinked a little, but it might have been the cold February breeze and the brisk ride here that had touched her cheeks with color.

"I haven't heard from him, no. I don't really think about Xav anymore," she said airily.

That was bad. His sister had mooned after Xav Phillips for so long Jace had begun to think she might actually manage to catch the man. But lately, he'd noticed his sister mentioning him less and less, and frequenting the canyons—where Xav had often ridden lookout duty—almost never.

It was a complete reversal for his baby sister, and he felt sorry for her. He knew too well what it felt like to love someone and not have that person return your feelings in the slightest. Or to pretend to return your feelings, while all the time crushing your heart with lies.

"You're the last Callahan," Jace told his sister. "The last free spirit in our family tree."

"I'll always be that way."

"Ash, I have no doubt that the right man will tie you down sooner rather than later. Not that I'm in a hurry to see my baby sister scooped up by a—"

"Jace, I don't want to talk about it," she interrupted, wheeling her horse around and kicking it into a full gallop back toward Rancho Diablo.

Whoa. She was hurting bad. He felt terrible about his awkward approach at comforting her. Jace wished he could fix it for her, force Xav Phillips to love her. But just like with him and Sawyer, love played out the way it was going to. You couldn't make another person love you.

Jace thought about his parents, and wondered how

they'd ever managed to find each other, fall in love, make their relationship work. Seven children, and then witness protection.

He thought about the cozy house in Colorado and felt a little peace. He, Galen, Dante, Tighe, Falcon, Sloan and Ash had done all right for themselves, thanks to the care of Running Bear and Fiona.

But it could have all turned out so much differently.

They'd been blessed. Fortunate. Watched over by angels or spirits, whatever one called the heavenly supernatural that guided them. So had their cousins, the Callahans, who now resided in Hell's Colony, Texas, until they could one day come back home.

When we've got this ranch locked down for our cousins, they can come back here, and we Chacon Callahans can go our way. Back to where we came from.

They really had no home, though. Home was where your family was.

His family was at Rancho Diablo: Sawyer and their children, Jason and Ashley. Jace smiled, thinking about his impending offspring. He'd felt them move inside Sawyer last night when he'd touched her stomach, almost afraid to make love to her. She'd urged him on, telling him it was fine. She'd whispered sweet words to him, tantalizing him, drawing him in.

The worst part was that he went into the trap so easily.

She was his family. He'd stay with her and the children no matter what.

No matter how much it hurt to know she might not be playing him straight.

JACE RODE BACK to the ranch slowly, deep in his thoughts, until he realized Fiona was waving frantically at him from the back porch. He rode toward her, his heart catching at her worried face.

"What is it?"

"I couldn't reach you on your cell! Sawyer's having stomach pains! She didn't want anyone to tell you, but you need to get her to the hospital *now!*"

He slid off his horse and handed it over to a groom, rushing past his aunt into the house and hurrying up the stairs. "Did anybody call the doctor?"

"Yes, but I think we're past Doc Cartwright now. She needs to go straight to the hospital!" Fiona's face was pale. "Galen's looking her over."

Jace went into Sawyer's room to find his brother in full physician mode, checking her heart rate, her pulse, gently trying to keep her calm. Sawyer looked up at Jace the moment he walked in the door.

"Jace! I think the babies are trying to come. It's too early!"

"It's okay," he said, trying to soothe her. He went to sit beside her. He noted the pain on his wife's face, glanced to read his brother's.

"Let's take her in," Galen said softly, and Jace's blood turned cold. Granted, his brother was no gynecologist, but he was a skilled general practitioner of allopathic and holistic medicine. If he said a hospital was required, then something was wrong.

"I'll get the car. Don't worry, babe, it's going to be fine." Jace kissed her and then hurried down the stairs.

Fiona and Burke had already pulled the family van around. Jace gratefully nodded and hurried inside to carry his wife down.

To his surprise, Sawyer was already downstairs, being

helped out of a walled-off pantry in the kitchen by Ash and Running Bear.

"What is this?" Jace demanded.

"A secret," Ash said. "A joint this large has hidden passageways, you know."

He glanced at the small elevator that had been disguised behind the wall he'd always thought held the locked and secret gun cabinet. There was no time to ask questions about this newest bit of Rancho Diablo information. Jace filed it away for later reference and scooped his wife up, carrying her to the van.

"I feel awful, Jace. My stomach hurts so badly."

Sawyer laid her head against his shoulder, and Jace's heart bled at the deep sadness and fear in her voice.

He'd brought this on her by making love to her last night. He shouldn't have; he'd known that deep in his heart. And yet, selfishly, he couldn't resist her.

He'd never been able to resist her. Which was what made him ripe for the fact he'd fallen for a woman who'd been working against his family.

That couldn't matter now. His children were in trouble. Sawyer's pale face scared the hell out of him.

He didn't know what he'd do if something happened to her. She'd become his very life.

Gently, he put Sawyer in the ranch van, and his sister and Fiona jumped in to comfort her as he sped toward the hospital, fearful that everything he loved most might be snatched away from him by the cruel winds of fate.

Chapter Nine

"Bed rest," the doctor pronounced after Sawyer had been thoroughly examined. "Absolute bed rest. I'll let you go home, because you've been stabilized for the moment with medication, but there'll be a nurse out to check on you tomorrow, and I don't want to hear that you've moved one inch from your bed. This is very serious," he told Sawyer. "I know you're used to a lot of activity, but you can consider yourself bedbound for now. It won't be forever, but it's important that we keep your babies inside you as long as we possibly can. The longer, the better," he emphasized one last time. "No stairs, no nothing. The nurse will come out and give you medication by IV if you have any further cramping."

"Thank you," Sawyer murmured, exhausted and frightened. She couldn't look at Jace's worried face again. His every thought was hidden behind a stoic expression, but she could read him every time he glanced at her.

He was afraid they'd endangered the babies.

She'd never be able to convince him that their love-making hadn't negatively affected her pregnancy. He wouldn't come near her now; that was clear in his stiff posture as he helped her slowly move to the wheelchair to be taken to the van.

Her husband had heard the doctor's warnings, and he wouldn't take any chances.

They already had too many things to regret. "Jace," she said, as he pushed her wheelchair down the hall. "The doctor said what we did last night probably didn't have anything to do with this."

He didn't say anything, just silently wheeled her to the van, which Fiona and Ash had brought around for them. The ladies hopped out to help her, and Sawyer felt silly and useless as she was assisted into the front passenger's seat.

Everything hurt more than she dared to let on. Already Jace looked as if he was ready to lash her to a bed and keep her in it, so she didn't say anything else as he closed the van door. A small tear threatened to fall from her eye, but she wouldn't allow herself to feel hurt over the sudden distance she was picking up from her husband.

She put a hand on her stomach, comforted by the doctor's words that everything would be fine as long as she rested. Didn't move.

Jace would be tied to her. He wouldn't want to let her out of his sight, which wasn't good for Rancho Diablo. As a one-time ranch employee, she knew that every person had their job and their role. Rancho Diablo had stayed out of Wolf's hands this long because all members of the family worked as a team.

She wasn't really part of the team.

But that didn't mean she wanted Jace having to stop his job to stand over her, guard her, for the rest of her pregnancy. She had every intention of keeping these babies inside her for at least the next two months.

"Jace," Sawyer said suddenly, "I'm going to stay at Uncle Storm's place. Not his town house, but his place you bought, next door to Rancho Diablo. Since he and Lu are staying there now, they can keep an eye on me. It makes sense for everybody involved."

He glanced at her. From the back of the van, there wasn't a peep. Fiona and Ash weren't going to say a word—and that was exactly why she'd brought up her request now. Jace was far less likely to deny her wishes with his sister and aunt hearing what Sawyer felt was best for herself and the babies.

And for Jace, if he only knew it.

"If that's what you want," he said, his tone remote, and she felt a dagger of sadness lacerate her heart. He'd given up easily, more easily than she'd imagined, and that was good.

The problem was, she didn't know if she could make him understand that it wasn't him she was running from this time.

JACE MOVED SAWYER into Storm Cash's place because that's what she wanted—not because he felt good about it. He didn't. A wife belonged with her husband, but Sawyer had made it clear more than once that she simply wasn't comfortable with him, and he supposed he couldn't blame her.

They'd been so far apart for so long that maybe there wasn't a way to bridge the gap. He knew she felt that he didn't trust her—what Callahan trusted a Cash, anyway?—and the truth was, anybody on the outside looking in would probably say Sawyer didn't deserve to be trusted.

He knew her better than she knew herself, though. She was the answer to everything he needed in his soul, and that made her good for Rancho Diablo.

"So now what?" Ash demanded when he returned to Rancho Diablo at midnight. His sister sat in the kitchen, perched on a bar stool like a fey elf, discreetly waiting up for him, probably. She pushed a cup of coffee his way and pointed to a plate of gingersnaps that were on the counter. "I advise that the two of you do *not* separate for two months, and then try to kiss and make up when the babies are born. Not that you asked my opinion. No one ever does."

He ruffled his sister's hair and sat down next to her. "Thanks for the joe."

"Don't sit down. There's a family meeting upstairs."

"Now?" He was exhausted, his mind consumed with Sawyer.

"Yep." Ash rose. "Pretty cool about the hidden passage, huh? Freaked you out a little."

He followed his giggling sister, carrying the plate of cookies and his mug with him. "If I got freaked out every time Rancho Diablo revealed one of its secrets, I'd have to go sit in the canyons and stare at cacti and mumble to myself."

"That's actually not a bad life. I wouldn't mind it," Ash said wistfully as they went upstairs. "I'm going to tell Galen tonight that he has to split Sister Wind Ranch with all of us, the big egghead."

"It's Loco Diablo, and Galen won't do it. You don't even have a family yet, and as we established, you're not ready to settle down. So you wouldn't be up for the ranch, anyway. Fiona's rules are clear."

"I'm a rule breaker. Haven't you figured that out yet?"

Ash pushed open the library door, ushering him by. The plate of cookies was promptly descended upon by his brothers. Tighe and Dante stuck their big paws in first, the latter tossing one to Galen.

"Like little piglets," Ash said with a sigh as Sloan reached to grab a few, and Falcon snagged the last. "Now that your munchies are satisfied, let business begin. Galen," Ash said. "We've got trouble around here. The place is crawling with reporters and Feds. I came across a treasure hunter the other day trespassing with one of those treasure-hunting rigs."

"Metal detector," Jace clarified.

"Not only did it detect metal," Ash said, "but this one could detect graves, hidden chambers, crypts and caves. Very sophisticated. You can imagine that I banished him from the property with all due haste." She looked around at them. "I would like to submit to all of you that we are outmanned and outgunned. We can't hold off Wolf's minions any longer. And we're a woman down."

Jace frowned. Sawyer wouldn't be on the job anytime soon, though she would excoriate him if she heard him say that. "Getting to the fact that you've recently revealed a hidden passage yourself—"

"That was Running Bear's doing," Ash said. "I didn't know about it, either. Fiona never mentioned the kitchen dumbwaiter elevator thing to me, though I'm sure she knows about it."

"What could the trespasser have been hunting?" Dante asked.

"Graves, hidden chambers, crypts and secret caves," Ash said, exasperated. "Weren't you listening, big brother?"

"What did he say he wanted, Ash?" Galen demanded. "And why didn't you tell us sooner?"

"Because." She shrugged. "We were kind of busy with

the babies and all. I'm an aunt first and a trespasser-hunter second. Besides, I kept his toy, so it didn't matter to me about the grave robber or whatever he was."

Jace stared at her, as dumbfounded as his brothers.

"What do you mean, you kept his toy?" Sloan demanded.

"He was happy to give it up, considering what I told him I'd do to him if he didn't. I acquired his fancy computer that went with it, too. It's quite an amazing doo-hickey." She went to a cabinet in the library and pulled out the equipment.

They all gathered around, eyeing the loot with astonishment.

"Ash, you can't just take someone's stuff," Jace said. "This is nice equipment."

"Can't I?" she retorted. "I think I did. Like I said, he was happy to give it up in return for me not reporting him to the sheriff or kicking the daylights out of him."

"Ash," Jace murmured, sitting her down on a leather sofa. His brothers followed him over, and they all looked down at their tiny sister. "Ash, you're the baby. You're not supposed to be this tough," he said, feeling a bit lost. "We kick the bad guys around, and the trespassers, and the other enemy. We want you to…"

He hesitated, and Ash glared up at her gang of brothers. "What? Comb my hair and put bows in it? Wear makeup? Heels?" She shook her head. "Sorry. I'm tougher than all of you and you know it. Without me, this team would be lost."

Someone passed around the crystal tumblers of whiskey, and Jace gladly took one. He was disturbed, but he couldn't exactly pinpoint why. Ash was being honest;

she'd always been tough. Most of the Callahan women were tough.

Not this tough.

He looked to Galen for advice. His oldest brother shrugged, and judging by the others' expressions, they were all stumped by Ash.

She rolled her eyes at all of them and then looked at Galen, as well.

"Galen, I move that you split the land across the canyons among all of us. Tonight. We're no longer hostage to Fiona's challenge. I have no plans to marry, and I deserve that land just as much as anyone in this room. I know Grandfather advised you to take the land to protect us from Wolf, but I can take care of myself." She looked around at her brothers. "It's a hotbed of smugglers and thieves who want to tear this place apart. I don't have time to think about getting married. All of you have children now, but I won't be having any. So I move that the challenge is over. Done. Finished."

Jace glanced at Galen again. "She's right," he said quietly. "She deserves her piece. In fact, we all deserve a home of our own. One day the Callahans will come back here, and that will be good. But our hearts are here now," he said, thinking about Sawyer. She'd told Storm the Callahans could return any day. Why had she said that?

And did it matter? She might be next door, but his heart was with her. If he had to pitch a tent and live in Storm's garden, he'd do that to be with his family.

"Actually," Galen said, "I have news to report about that land. The Feds have discovered that it's so overrun by tunnels and smugglers that it's barely inhabitable."

"Fine," Ash said. "We'll fill in the tunnels and build an

enormous amusement park. Shops and a mall. It wouldn't hurt us to have a different livelihood, and commercial real estate would suit me just fine. I'm sick to death of horses and oil wells and cows and those stupid peacocks out front. I haven't seen the Diablos in weeks, and that's very, very bad, as every single one of you know. It means we've *failed* at our mission. And that Wolf has won." She looked at Jace. "I'm sorry to dump all this on you right now. We should be throwing you a wedding party, and helping you figure out where your baby nursery is going to be. I feel sorry for you and Sawyer, but we're in a deep hole here."

Jace shrugged. "I doubt Sawyer wants anything more than going to term with the babies. We'll figure out the nursery and other details later." She wasn't even wearing the ring he'd given her. He'd hoped that the lovely ring would be a peace offering, a silent commitment to the depth of his feelings for her, but he hadn't seen it since he'd left it in her room.

"Ash is right," he continued. "They're coming. No doubt they're already here. Which means no one is safe. Wolf has outmaneuvered us. He just had more people, more resources. And maybe we never understood the blackness of our uncle's heart. But the Diablos haven't been around in a long time, and that is a very bad sign."

They all looked silently at each other.

"If we divide the land," Jace said suddenly, "it will be tough for Wolf to take it from us. Too many pieces to chase down."

"True," Galen said. "Vote?"

All hands went up. Ash grinned, triumphant. "All right, brothers," she said, standing, "we'll draw for the spaces. I'm not afraid of my stupid uncle, and I'm ready to pitch my tent there now. Tonight." She glanced around at them, and Jace thought his sister looked a little wild, a bit untamed.

"I'm not giving up on the only place I have to call home," she said. "It's been a long time since any of us had a place we could call our own. Besides the stone fire ring near the canyons, which Running Bear gave to us when we first came, we've had nothing, no stake that is ours. I will burn Uncle Wolf out before I allow him to take one square inch of what's mine."

She went out the door, and Jace and his brothers looked at each other.

"Wow," Tighe said, "little sister's got a burr under her saddle."

"It's gotten to her," Falcon said. "This job could get to anyone. We're losing, and she knows it. It's eating at her. It sucks to feel helpless."

"Damn it," Jace muttered. "We can't let Wolf get us down. There's too much at stake." He stood and addressed the room. "It's been months since we've seen the Diablos. We knew Wolf's intent was to get to them—that was why they were tunneling from Loco Diablo to here. First, to get to us from a different vantage point, and second, to take out the spirit of Rancho Diablo. The Diablos, the heart and soul of the place. Wolf knows only too well that his father's spirit—Running Bear's spirit—is in the mustangs. Without them, Grandfather will be weakened. Rancho Diablo will be seriously weakened, as well." *And we'll be lost.*

"We'll be lost," Dante said, echoing his thoughts, and Jace knew his brothers saw the situation the same way he did.

"And this bone-digging toy," Jace said, going over to

study what his sister had commandeered, "tells me that we're not the only ones aware that there may be hidden caves under Rancho Diablo. Tunnels."

"Depositories," Sloan said.

"Spirits," Galen added.

"We knew that the smugglers had dug under Loco Diablo, and we knew they hadn't quite reached here, nor the canyons. Not then," Jace said. "But I never thought about hidden caves, or buried treasure here. Except for what's in the basement."

They all looked at him.

"It's secret," Galen said. "It's the Callahan buried silver treasure."

"But," Jace said, "Wolf wouldn't be sending men over here with treasure-hunting devices if he didn't think there was silver and something much more important buried somewhere under Rancho Diablo."

"Like what?" Falcon demanded.

He wasn't certain. Prickles ran over his arms, though he was warm enough in his winter clothes. He thought about the cozy house in Colorado, and the sense he'd had that there were spirits there that he recognized, happy memories he'd once known. Remembered well, deep in his heart.

"Wolf's too close," he said. "He knows something we don't know. And it has to do with the tunnels under Loco Diablo."

"Sister Wind Ranch," Ash said, sailing back into the room. "When are you lunkheads ever going to figure out that land has a feminine spirit?"

They all stared at her. She wore black from head to toe, combat fatigue style. Heavy boots, a black jacket.

"What the hell are you doing?" Jace demanded. "You look like you're about to go grave-robbing."

"I am. And you're coming with me. But first," Ash said, zipping up her jacket, "we're going to go ask your wife where her uncle hid the information we need."

Chapter Ten

Sawyer didn't like being on bed rest, but she couldn't really complain because she felt so much better. The cramps were gone and the babies seemed settled. The nurse would be out early tomorrow morning to check on her. She'd had Jace place her recliner next to the window so she could keep an eye on Rancho Diablo.

And Jace, of course.

She missed the daily jolt of adrenaline that came with working at Rancho Diablo. There was always something happening, and not being part of the action was hard. On the other hand, in a couple of months she'd have two beautiful babies.

"I can lie very still for sixty days," she told herself, picking up her binoculars. She looked through them toward Rancho Diablo, watching a truck go down the long drive toward the main road.

It turned up the road that led to Storm's house. Sawyer peered more closely, not altogether surprised to see Ash and Jace get out and head toward the porch. The doorbell rang.

"Come in! It's unlocked!"

Her big husband walked in, wearing a glare—his normal expression these days.

"Why is the front door unlocked?" he demanded.

Ash looked at her sympathetically.

"Because I can't get out of this chair, and Uncle Storm and Lu went into town to fetch some groceries." Sawyer frowned at Jace. "I can't get up to answer the door, obviously."

"You shouldn't be having any visitors, and the front door should be locked. Every window and every door of this house should be locked."

"Well, it is your house," she replied, "so I guess you can make the rules." She shrugged at Jace.

"I'm not telling you what to do, babe. I'm worried about you. You know it's not safe. Unlocked doors aren't a good idea," he said patiently.

She hated it when he was patient with her, especially when she knew she was being cranky. "Hi, Ash."

"Hi, Sawyer." Ash sat down next to her. "What can I do to help?"

Sawyer sighed. "Explain to Jace that pregnant doesn't mean helpless."

Ash smiled, glanced at her brother. "Let's not try to explain things that are beyond his comprehension."

"Hey," Jace said. "I get it. I just don't like it."

Sawyer nodded. "I figured that out. So, why am I getting a family visit?"

He leaned against the wall, and she let her gaze run over him, studying him in his worn jeans, scuffed boots, black thermal shirt and sheepskin jacket. Looking at him never failed to get her heart beating faster.

"Sawyer," Ash said, and Sawyer turned at the strangely patient tone in her sister-in-law's voice. "Did Storm give you some information about Sister Wind Ranch? That land he sold to us?"

Sawyer looked at Jace, who shrugged.

"Uncle Storm didn't say much about it, except that he wished he hadn't bought it. He was happy to get it off his hands. Said it was far too large a spread for him, and that he wished he'd never allowed Wolf to talk him into buying it."

"Why did Wolf want your uncle to buy the land we call Loco Diablo?" Jace asked.

"Wolf told my uncle that if your family bought the land, you'd basically own the county. Your power would exponentially multiply. Like a conglomerate, or a Mafia family. Wolf said he felt like he was being pushed out of the family business, which he had every right to be in, and would be in except that his father, Running Bear, didn't like him."

"So he wanted Storm to be a counterweight?" Jace asked. "Spread the power around?"

She nodded. "And Wolf offered my uncle protection if he bought it. All the bad things that were happening wouldn't happen here, to his land. Uncle didn't really know what that meant, but he said it wasn't his place to get involved in family issues. He didn't know who the bad guys were, who the good guys were. So he agreed to purchase the land from the elderly gentleman who owned it. He got a great price on the deal."

"Why would the former owner do that?" Ash demanded. "Why sell for a low price when he could have sold to any developer for more? Or to us?"

"Because your uncle Wolf told the old man he'd make his life a misery if he didn't do the deal just the way he wanted him to," Sawyer said, her gaze on Jace.

"Why didn't you tell me this before now?" he asked.

"I'm a bodyguard, not a business manager." Sawyer

frowned. "Besides, Wolf is your uncle. I figured you already knew."

"Why did you come to work for us?" Jace knelt down next to her chair, put his hand on her stomach. The babies kicked as if they knew their father was holding them.

"I already told you. My uncle wasn't certain what was going on." Sawyer looked into Jace's eyes, wishing they didn't have to talk about this again. It brought up all the sore spots in their marriage, the lack of trust, the strained feelings. "He wanted me to find out what I could."

"He should have known," Ash said. "He'd done business with Fiona."

"Horse trading is a different thing, and that was many years ago. He had no great knowledge of the Chacon Callahans. Besides, Wolf was telling some pretty crazy stories about you." Sawyer shook her head. "It didn't take me long to figure out he was evil. And at that point, I knew I would do everything I could to help you."

Jace studied her, his eyes searching hers.

"I believe you," he said.

"Thank you." It meant so much to her.

"I think my uncle must have given your uncle something," Jace said. "Wolf was trying to protect his smuggling operation, and he was using your uncle to divert us by buying Loco Diablo. So when Storm bought the land, he had to have gotten something from Wolf for doing so."

Sawyer's eyes widened with surprise and dismay. "Are you suggesting my uncle accepted a bribe to do it? Beyond Wolf's promise to put his men to protecting my uncle's spread from the trouble that was occurring between you and your uncle?"

"Yes," Jace said simply. "I'm saying Storm had to have been given something of value to do what he did."

"Like what?" Sawyer demanded. "I assure you Uncle Storm's goal was getting distance from the lot of you and whatever was going on with your uncle."

Jace glanced at Ash, who seemed to understand his question. "Financial assistance," Ash murmured.

"I don't think my uncle needs money," Sawyer snapped.

Jace moved his hand to hers. "Maybe to buy Loco Diablo, he did. There were surveyors who would have needed to be bought off, plus palms to be crossed with silver at the state level, so they would look the other way at such a big land deal. Deeds to change hands. It all happened very quickly, and would have required funding."

Sawyer felt herself getting angry with Jace, and disgusted. She couldn't understand how the man could live with so much conceit. "You really think you're the only people in New Mexico who can run a spread? My uncle has always owned land. Cattle, horses, whatever. He didn't need a bribe."

"Not a bribe so much as assistance. Maybe a sort of silent partnership. An angel investor," Jace said. "You can't think of anything of value your uncle recently acquired?"

She was almost too mad to think. She glared at him, then at Ash, who was watching her without emotion. These people were supposed to be her family! "The only thing my uncle has gotten lately is a town house in Diablo and a new wife. He sold his ranch to you, and the land you call Loco Diablo. What else do you want from him? You got everything he had," she said bitterly. "All because of the feud between you and your uncle."

"I found someone near the canyons with a metal detector, a very sophisticated setup," Ash said. "He was looking for something."

Sawyer sighed. "Okay, I'll bite. What was he looking for?"

"He said he was looking for a graveyard," Ash said. "A graveyard that was rumored to have treasure beyond imagination. I told him that was nonsense, and sent him and his two buddies on their way, of course."

"What has that got to do with my uncle?"

Jace stood, crossed to a window, looked out toward Rancho Diablo before turning to face her again. Sawyer's heart skipped a beat.

"You think my uncle knows where this graveyard is," Sawyer said. "You think Wolf told him to help him find it, and agreed to split treasure with him if he could help him get Rancho Diablo away from the Callahans. You think that's why his gang is always trespassing. And," she said, realization dawning, "that Uncle Storm sent me to work for you to find out anything I could. And of course, I romanced you as part of the grand plan."

"Not so fast," Jace said. "We're just asking if there's anything Wolf ever gave your uncle. It's a hunch, nothing more."

"I got suspicious when the man with the equipment mentioned your uncle," Ash said. "He seemed to know Storm and Wolf pretty well, for an out-of-towner. This made me curious, so I looked the man up. Turns out he's no small-time treasure hobbyist. He's a well-known treasure seeker with a military background. In other words, he's a kind of bounty hunter. He specializes in buried treasure, and dead bodies instead of live ones."

Sawyer sucked in a breath. "You're absolutely crazy if you think my uncle sent that man to scout your property."

"He didn't," Jace said. "Wolf sent him. But you've admitted yourself that—"

"My uncle asked me to hire on at Rancho Diablo to find out what I could about your feud." Sawyer nodded. "Yes, he did. I've admitted that. But he never once mentioned anything to me about a hidden graveyard or buried treasure." She was more hurt than she could have ever imagined. Looking at Jace was too heartbreaking. Not only did he not trust her, but he thought she was part of a plot to steal his family's wealth. Sawyer put her head back against the recliner and closed her eyes. "I'm tired," she said, so drained she could barely keep her eyes open anymore. "Please leave."

Jace walked over, touched her hand. She snatched it away, not opening her eyes.

After a moment, she heard the front door open.

"I'll be back to check on you later," Jace said, but she didn't answer. The door closed, and she wiped her eyes, thankful no tears had fallen while he was around to witness them. She wouldn't let him see how much he'd hurt her. What a ridiculous thing to ask. Of course her uncle hadn't taken a bribe from Wolf! All he'd wanted was to stay out of the fracas between Wolf and the Callahans. He'd wanted protection for his land.

The worst part was how much she loved Jace. She was madly in love with him, had been for a long time. But he would never see her that way. There would always be seeds of distrust between them.

The only things holding her and Jace together now were these babies. She placed both hands around her stomach with a touch of sadness.

Babies who would grow up with a father and a mother who didn't love each other, didn't even trust each other.

Sawyer opened her eyes, gazed out toward Rancho Diablo, her heart breaking. Dusk stole over the ranch as the sun retreated, layering the seven-chimneyed house in the distance with a fairy-tale glow. How many times had she looked out on that castlelike structure, wishing she could be part of a family like the Callahans? And then when she'd gotten the job there, how fortunate she'd felt to finally be part of that world! She'd never awakened without feeling a shiver of joy that she was at Rancho Diablo, trusted with Callahan children and lives, part of an extraordinary world that was envied by everyone.

And then somehow, miraculously, a Callahan man had seemed to fall in love with her.

But the fairy tale hadn't exactly turned out the way she'd dreamed.

"I BELIEVE HER," Jace said to Ash as they returned to Rancho Diablo.

"I do, too." His sister shook her head. "I'm missing a huge piece of the puzzle somehow. Storm has to know something. He must know what Wolf's true purpose is."

"Or maybe not," Jace said, struck by a sudden thought about the two men who'd followed them out to Vegas, the knife in the cake, and the two men with the treasure hunter. "Maybe Uncle Wolf sent that man with the metal detector to hunt for what he thinks is here, not what he's got. Maybe Wolf used Storm and never intended to share any treasure with him."

"Something made Storm jump and buy that land, and it wasn't the sudden desire to own twenty thousand additional acres, not at his age. Come on, Jace, what was Storm going to do with that much land? He's got a small spread and a house, some livestock. He's done well in horse trading and breeding, but he's hardly a mover and shaker."

"True." Jace ruminated on the strange turn of events, all the while trying to keep his mind off his delicate, pregnant wife, who by now was deeply unhappy with him and had every right to be. "My wife's not with me."

"You're going to have to fix that. I don't think she preferred your Sherlock Holmes approach. It was kind of meat-headed."

Jace glanced at his sister. "Thank you for your support. Especially since it was your idea."

"Indeed," Ash said. "However, I can't do everything for you. Your approach should have been more groveling. More loverlike. Sweetheart," she said, her voice cooing, as she showed her brother how to speak to a lady, "can you think of anything my mean ol' uncle might have held over your honest and courageous uncle's head? Like a map, or a plat, of—"

"I get it," Jace said, interrupting her soliloquy. "I'll have to figure out a way to dig myself out of trouble." It wouldn't be easy. Sawyer had every right to think he was the world's biggest rat.

He hated feeling like a rat when he wanted to be a conquering hero. "Damn," he muttered, "I'm ready for Wolf and his men to fall off a cliff and disappear."

"The problem is, Wolf's got the cartel breathing down his neck, I'm sure of it. They want revenge on our parents, and the Callahan parents—and Wolf wants Rancho Diablo and all its treasure."

Of which there was a lot. Running Bear and Jeremiah Callahan, and even Jace's own father and mother, Carlos and Julia, had been astute and frugal, with a vision that had built this ranch. They'd breathed Rancho Diablo to life, put their hearts and souls into every inch. With Fiona's, Burke's and Running Bear's competent overseeing, Rancho Diablo was a fine example of a successful working ranch. Join Loco Diablo to Rancho Diablo and Dark Diablo, and there was no question why Wolf would be envious.

"I wonder what happened between Running Bear and his son to get them crosswise with each other," Jace murmured. He vowed to have the best relationship he possibly could with his son and daughter. In fact, he couldn't wait to hold them in his arms.

He couldn't wait to hold Sawyer, either, but that probably wasn't going to happen anytime soon.

"Running Bear says Wolf was always different. That of his three sons, that one was a bad apple. The other two understood service and the spirit of a life bigger than themselves. They understood they were strong and blessed, and they could share those gifts with others." Ash shrugged. "Wolf, Grandfather said, was stubborn and jealous from early on. No matter how he tried to help his son, he couldn't get him to understand that the spirit inside is the real treasure. That a person can nourish their soul with good, or succumb to the darkness of negativity and envy. Wolf wanted things to be easier than they could be."

Jace grunted. "I'm going to be an excellent father to Jason and Ashley."

Ash perked up. "Ashley?"

"Yes." He grinned at her hopeful look. "That was Sawyer's choice. She wanted to name our little girl after you."

A grin split Ash's face. "I always knew I liked Sawyer!"

He laughed at his sister's change of tune. "I like her, too. I'd better go see if I can convince her that she likes me back."

"Yes, you should. You were pretty hard on her, you know," Ash said, heading inside the house. "I'm going to go tell everyone that I have a namesake. It's called bragging, and I have it coming to me."

"Ash."

She turned around at his call. "Yes?"

"Don't confront any more trespassers in the canyons by yourself."

She raised a brow. "Brother, I'm never alone."

"You were by yourself. Something could have happened." He hated to think of his little sister alone in the canyons. "You're not even supposed to be out there by yourself, as you know. Galen's orders."

"Galen is wonderful about throwing orders around, as are you." Ash blew him a kiss. "No worries, brother. Like I said, I'm never alone."

She went inside, and Jace sighed. "She doesn't listen," he muttered. "It's like talking to the wind."

He hoped Sawyer would listen better.

To Jace's dismay, Sawyer was being trundled off by an EMT when he returned to the house next door. "What the hell is going on?" he demanded, fear leaping inside him.

"Her blood pressure is high, and her vital signs worry me. She's cramping again," the visiting nurse informed him.

He knew Sally Clausen. He'd met her at some of Fiona's Books'n'Bingo soirees and charity functions. Sally was gray-haired, practical and thorough. If she'd reported her concerns to the doctor and had been told to send Sawyer to the hospital, something was dreadfully wrong.

He strode to Sawyer's side. "What can I do for you, babe?"

She was so pale, lying there on the gurney. "I don't know. The cramps came back after you left. Fortunately, Sally was scheduled to come by and check on me." Sawyer's blue eyes stared up at him. "I'm so scared, Jace."

He understood. He was terrified. "You're going to be fine. The babies are going to be fine." This was his fault, of course. He'd upset her, raised her blood pressure, when she was supposed to be resting.

What a crappy husband he was turning out to be.

"I'll ride with you."

Sawyer barely nodded. "Thank you."

He texted Ash. Follow me over to the hospital with a truck.

Instantly, his phone buzzed back. Are we having babies today? read her text.

He hoped not. The babies needed more time. He swallowed hard and followed the EMTs as they took Sawyer to the ambulance. He got in, held her hand and told himself everything was going to be just fine.

Somehow.

Chapter Eleven

"My poor brother!" Ash rushed into the hospital thirty minutes later, hugging Jace when she found him in the waiting room. They wouldn't allow him to go back to see his wife—not yet.

Apparently, Sawyer had told the doctor she wanted to be alone for now.

He couldn't blame her—but he was dying inside.

"I'll be all right."

Ash's eyes were wide. "It was bad juju to ask about her uncle."

"Ash, it wasn't bad juju. It's just going to be a tough pregnancy for her, I suppose. It will all work out." He hugged his sister tighter, trying to alleviate her worries.

"You don't have a nursery set up."

"This is true. If the babies come early, we'll be in a bit of a hurry to get things done. But we'll do it." He wasn't really worried about that, though. They had enough family around with cribs and baby paraphernalia they could borrow.

The thing was, he and Sawyer didn't have a home for them and their family.

"Where will you live?" Ash asked.

"That's a question for another day." He swallowed

hard, wondering how he could talk Sawyer into living with him.

Ash slumped in a chair. "I feel so guilty."

"That's not like you." He sat next to her. "No negative vibes."

"It's not doing me much good," she admitted. "I'm never having children."

He laughed out loud. "Ash, you'll have children. And no doubt they'll be the toughest kids around. They'll be born untamed, like their mother."

"I think I'd make a better aunt than a mother. And besides, my children would be plenty tame. They're not going to live like we did," she said, her voice turning a bit dreamy. "If I had children, they'd have ballet lessons."

"Even the boys?" he teased.

"If they want," she said. "And my girls will have long, silky hair that I put lots of bows in." She ran her fingers through her hair, which had grown from a short boy cut convenient for military life to a shoulder-length fall of silvery-blond strands. "And they would always have a store-bought birthday cake. Unless Fiona's around to make it. I'm no good with baking."

He listened to his sister's dreams, letting her voice soothe him, keep his mind off what was happening with Sawyer. His gut wouldn't unknot. He'd never been this scared in his life, not when he was deployed, not even when their parents had gone away.

That had been a terrible day. But just like Ash, he had dreams for his children.

He dreamed that his two babies would live in a house with their mother and father, who would never have to leave. They'd always be together, a family.

Those were his dreams.

"IT HAD NOTHING to do with you, Jace." Sawyer hated the fearful look on her husband's face. After the doctor had ordered extra medication for her, she'd allowed Jace to join her. The nurse had said he was like a caged panther in the waiting room, and Sawyer had taken pity on him. "I guess I have a small frame. There's not much room. Or it's just my body's reactions. But I wasn't stressed about you and Ash asking me those questions. Irritated, but not stressed."

"Let's not talk about that anymore." He paced around the room, unable to relax. "You just rest."

She closed her eyes for a moment, too keyed up to relax. The whole incident had been so frightening.

Sawyer opened her eyes again. "I don't know that I'll be able to carry to term. Not even until April."

"I'll hire on extra help. I don't want you to lift a pinkie." Jace sat on the bed next to her and took her hand. "If you could have anything on the planet that would make your pregnancy easier and better, what would it be? I want you to have everything you need."

She looked at her husband. That was an easy answer. She wanted him. But if she said that, Jace would say she had him.

Yet she didn't, not really. And she knew that. No relationship could survive the way theirs had begun, with all the trouble that had followed their impetuous wedding.

"Whatever you want, I'll get it for you," he promised. He put a hand on her tummy, smiled when he felt the babies jostling for space. "Clearly, they're not fazed by the day's events."

"They're always active. They use my body as a trampoline."

"You're beautiful," Jace told her, sweeping her hair

away from her face and kissing her lips. "I know you probably don't want me kissing you. I know you think I'm the world's biggest louse, or a traitor, or something."

"Not the world's biggest louse." She smiled, but he didn't smile back.

"We've got to have a home, babe."

She blinked. "I can't think about that right now."

"I know you can't. Let me think about it for you."

Suddenly, she liked the idea of Jace making the decisions—anybody making the decisions. It wasn't in her to be passive, but she suddenly felt so tired. Too tired even to hold him on the opposite side of the fence she tried to keep up between them. "We'll never be safe, wherever we go. It's never going to feel like a real home."

His hand tightened on hers.

"The thing is," she said softly, "we'd probably be better off with a divide-and-conquer strategy. Then the babies would be safer."

"Divide and conquer?" He sounded doubtful.

"Yes. We could have two houses, so no one can monitor the children easily. We won't keep to a steady routine that could be noticed."

"Don't think about it, Sawyer."

She looked at him. "My uncle became afraid of your uncle, Jace. He said he threatened him. How can I not think about my children being a kidnapping threat when it's happened in your family before?"

He shook his head. "I don't know. But I'll place a bodyguard outside your room."

"Oh, I'm not scared," Sawyer said. "Not now. I'm big as a house. I couldn't be moved unless someone brings a van and a pulley."

He smiled. "I'm going to lie next to my wife and scandalize the nurses."

She wriggled over. "There really isn't much scooting I can do. I'm almost bigger than the bed."

"Bet I can find some room."

She giggled when he squeezed up next to her, put a comforting hand over her stomach. "That feels wonderful," she said, sighing.

"That's right. Just call me Wonderful Callahan. Now go to sleep. As soon as the doctor springs you, I'm taking you back to Rancho Diablo. And you're not getting out of my sight again, little fireball of a wife."

"Hardly little."

"You're sassy and fun-sized in my book. I find the extra curves enticing. In fact, it's killing me not to explore them."

He was trying to make her feel better, and for that, he was a hero. There was nothing sexy or "fun-sized" about her now, but it was sweet of him to say so.

Sawyer rested her head on Jace's shoulder and tried not to think about the fact that Wolf had called her today. Right after that awful conversation with him, she'd begun cramping. Had felt terrible. Fear such as she'd never known had sliced into her.

Wolf had told her she was going to be sorry she'd ever worked for the Callahans, married one, was having Callahan children. He'd spent years making the Callahan parents disappear, and he could do that with her and her children, too.

Unless she told him everything she knew about the Callahans.

He'd even silkily threatened Uncle Storm and Lu,

making sure she understood just how much was riding on her decision.

She shivered, and Jace held her tighter.

"What's wrong? Is it the babies?" he asked.

"It's nothing. I was cold, but now I'm not."

His arms felt good, wrapped around her. Right now she could believe that she was safe, and that her children were safe.

Just for tonight, she'd let herself cling to that dream.

JACE'S WORLD TURNED upside down when Sawyer insisted on being moved to a small duplex in town, conveniently located next to the main street of Diablo, not much more than a block from Sheriff Cartwright's jail and the courthouse. The other side of the duplex was rented by Storm and Lu.

Apparently, the three of them had been in cahoots. Jace sensed that a plan had been forged, one that didn't include him.

He realized he wasn't far off when his wife told him he wasn't moving in with her.

"Yes, I am," Jace said. "Where you and my children go, I am. Pretty much like your shadow."

"No, Jace." Ensconced on a pretty floral sofa Lu had ordered for her while Sawyer was at the hospital, she gave him a look that didn't seem exactly welcoming. "I need to be alone."

"Being alone is the last thing you need." He frowned and went to perch on the edge of the sofa, so he could read her eyes as she talked. He could feel her trying to put distance between them, but he was a master at putting distance between himself and things that made him uncomfortable, so he knew exactly what his little fireball was up to. "It's no good. I'm staying right here in this tiny domicile with you." He glanced around. "The four of us will be nice and cozy."

"Jace, listen to me." Sawyer took a deep breath, holding her hand against her stomach for a moment. "You need to be at the ranch. I need to be closer in town, where Sally doesn't have to drive out so far to check my vitals and give me my drip. I'm absolutely determined to do this exactly by doctor's orders, and by being here, I'm nearer to everything."

"That's fine. I'll drive in."

"I don't want you to."

He looked at his stubborn wife. "What is going on with you, beautiful?"

"Exactly what I told you. It's better for me to be in town."

He got up, looked out the window. "Are you renting this place, or did you buy it?"

"You'd have to ask Uncle Storm. He took care of everything. I just told him I wanted to live in town. He and Lu decided it was best if I had family staying with me, and this duplex keeps us close, yet with privacy, according to him."

"I'm your family," Jace said, an uncomfortable prickle teasing his senses. He couldn't say that Sawyer had ever been an enthusiastic bride—he'd practically had to drag her to Vegas—but he began to wonder if she planned on keeping him as far away from her and the babies as possible. "I'm your family, and I can care for my wife just fine. Although Lu and Storm are always welcome, I plan on taking very good care of you."

"That's nice," she said, her tone careful, "except I don't want that, Jace."

She hadn't protested his presence when she'd been at the hospital. He combed his mind for anything that might have happened between then and now, only a few days later. "Look, I know you're worried—"

"Yes, and having time to myself is the best way for me to relax." She looked at him. "I'm going to live alone."

"It's Wolf, isn't it?" Jace asked, hit by a sudden thought. "You're afraid to stay at the ranch or Storm's. If you're here in town, you think you're safer. You're practically within shouting distance of Sheriff Cartwright's office."

She looked away. "I'm a little tired. I'm going to take a nap."

She was shutting him out. He could feel her withdrawal from him so clearly. "It doesn't feel honest," he said, leaning against a wall.

Sawyer looked up at him warily. "What doesn't feel honest?"

"You trying to run me off, when you spent so many months—more than a year, if we want to get technical—chasing me." He crossed his arms, stared at his wife, a little amused. "It's dishonest."

"I'm sorry you feel that way." She sent him a glare to show him she wasn't sorry at all, but he wasn't buying any of her story.

Yet he didn't want to push her, not when she was home from the hospital after a scare. Whatever was bugging his little wife would have to wait. Jace studied her, thinking how pretty she looked in a rose-colored maternity dress, snuggled on the floral sofa with a soft white throw across her lap. She looked like a princess—even though she said she was as big as a house.

Something didn't make sense. "I'm going to go. I need to get back because I'm riding canyon tonight, but—"

"Canyon!" Sawyer stared at him. "You have canyon duty?"

He shrugged. "We all take turns doing it. All seven of us, and Xav Phillips when he's around, keep an eye on what's going on over there, especially now that the new land purchase is pretty overrun with strangers and law enforcement." Jace looked at his wife curiously. "Why?"

"It just surprises me."

"You know Wolf's been trying to get onto the ranch for a long time. We're making sure that Rancho Diablo stays secure, but it's not easy now that there are reporters and Feds everywhere. We're constantly looking to make certain that none of Wolf's people manage to sneak onto Rancho Diablo under the guise that they're with the law or reporters." He shrugged. "I wouldn't put it past them to try."

"I really wish you didn't have to do canyon duty." Sawyer looked out the window, to all appearances unperturbed. Yet he sensed she wasn't as casual as she appeared. "Maybe Ash could go with you."

"Ash is hanging out with Fiona and Burke. They wouldn't like to think that they're part of the coverage, but we all agree Fiona's always going to be a target. She's pretty much the proverbial rock in Wolf's boot."

Sawyer didn't look at him. Jace was having trouble reading her. "I'll text you later, check in on you."

"Not if you're in the canyons. You won't have cell service." She finally looked up at him. "Trade off with one of your brothers tonight, Jace."

"Why?" He was completely surprised by her request.

"The canyons are dangerous."

"No more than the rest of Rancho Diablo." He opened the front door. "I'll text you in the morning. I don't want to call in case you're asleep."

She lowered her gaze, pressed her lips together as if she wanted to say more but wouldn't allow herself. "All right," she finally said, and he nodded and went out.

When he glanced back toward the window where her floral sofa was situated, he saw her watching him. He waved, and she waved back once—then disappeared from the window.

Frowning, Jace got in the truck and drove away.

SAWYER WAS FRANTIC. The last thing Jace needed to do was ride the canyon tonight. After Wolf's warning to her, she knew Jace could easily get picked off.

"This pregnancy stuff is not for the faint of heart," she muttered, reaching for her cell phone and dialing up the one person she could count on to help her.

Maybe.

Chapter Twelve

Thirty minutes later, Ash walked in, with Fiona at her side.

"I brought backup," Ash said. "The redoubtable aunt usually has a word of wisdom or two."

"More than two," Fiona said with asperity. "And I want to see what we've got to work with as far as a nursery is concerned." She hugged Sawyer, holding her close. "How are you, my dear? That was quite a scare you had."

Sawyer allowed herself to bathe in the Callahan kindness for a moment before stiffening her courage. "It was a scare, but I'm much better now. Thank you."

Fiona and Ash sat on chairs across from her, and Fiona placed a plate of cookies on the coffee table between them. She glanced around the room, which was bare of pictures, knickknacks and personal effects. "So what is this assistance you require? Decorating help, no doubt? You can't do much in your condition. We don't want you to move even your toes."

"It's a dilemma, really, and I need your advice."

Fiona leaned closer, her eyes bird-bright. "Advice is my favorite thing to give."

Ash laughed. "She's serious, too. So feel free to get started."

Sawyer feared that telling everything that was on her mind would cost her goodwill points with her new family, but she had to do it to keep her husband safe. And the Callahans. "I've thought long and hard about this, but there's no other way to do it than to just clear my conscience."

"Gracious," Fiona said, "this doesn't sound like you want tips on decorating a nursery in a tiny apartment." She glanced around, clearly finding the small, vintage duplex not completely to her liking. "You're making me feel like a cup of tea may be in order."

"I don't have any dishes or a teapot. Yet," Sawyer said hastily. "I'm so sorry I can't offer you anything more than a bottle of water."

Fiona sniffed. "Jace warned us as to the conditions. We came prepared. Ash, if you wouldn't mind?"

Her new sister-in-law smiled. "Sawyer, I hope you're ready for busybodying to the max."

"I don't know what you mean, niece," Fiona said. "Please bring in the housewarming gift."

Ash went out the door. Fiona looked at Sawyer. "While we're alone, I should tell you that I already know what you're going to say."

"You do?"

"Yes, I do. You don't have to do this," Fiona told her. "You're one of us now, and nothing that came before matters."

Sawyer felt her worry melt a little in the face of such consideration. "Thank you, but I really need to get it all out of my system."

"I figured you'd feel that way. Just remember, then, that on the other side of confession lays peace. We don't judge. Unless it's Wolf. Then I myself enjoy being judgmental."

Sawyer couldn't help smiling. "You're trying to make me feel better."

"It's working, too, isn't it?" Fiona demanded with a wink.

"It actually is." Yet Sawyer still felt guilty.

Ash came inside, shopping bags hanging from her arms. "I hope you don't mind that my aunt selected the decorating colors and scheme for your new home."

"Well, Sawyer doesn't have time to do it," Fiona said, her tone practical. "She has to concentrate on staying strong for the babies."

Ash set the shopping bags in front of Sawyer. "Please feel free to keep what you like. We'll take the rest back."

Sawyer pulled out a silver teakettle, pleased. "How nice! Fiona, will you do the honors?"

"Gladly." She went into the small kitchen and set the kettle on to boil as Sawyer pulled out darling white and light blue dish towels and cloth napkins. A braided rug for the entrance, and a welcome mat for the front porch. "I didn't know how much stuff you could possibly have accumulated during the years you worked as a bodyguard, so I took the liberty of picking out a few things for a small housewarming gift," she called from the kitchen. "Every well-run, cozy home must have a teakettle and teapot, in my opinion."

"And heaven knows, her opinion runs everything," Ash whispered. "I'll take back what you don't want."

Sawyer pulled soft tan towels from a bag. "I love it all. It's starting to feel more like home."

"Have you found the teapot yet?" Fiona called. "I'm ready for it."

Sawyer reached into the final bag, pulled out a delicate

white pot with pretty flowers curling around the base. "This is so sweet. You shouldn't have done so much."

"I should have if I'm going to be here watching babies. I have to have my comforts," Fiona said, taking the teapot into the kitchen. "Although I wish you hadn't moved so far away from the ranch. Still, I understand, I guess. I'll wash this up, and then tea is served. Then we can get down to business."

Ash looked at her. "Whatever you have to tell us, just know that we'll do anything to help. The most important thing is that you concentrate on your health. And my niece and nephew," she said, pleased.

"It's difficult," Sawyer admitted. "This isn't the easiest conversation I've ever had."

Fiona came back in and sat down. "Now, how can we help you?"

Sawyer swallowed. "Ash, you remember when you asked me the other day what my uncle might be hiding?"

Fiona glanced at Ash. "Ashlyn Chacon Callahan! You didn't say that to Sawyer!"

"It's okay," Sawyer said quickly. "I don't think my uncle's hiding anything, but Wolf called me."

"Wolf!" Fiona shook her head. "You hung up on him right away, I hope! And tell Jace. He'll know what to do about Wolf."

"No, no," Sawyer said. "That's exactly what I don't want. I don't want Jace doing anything. In fact, I'm swearing you both to secrecy." The last thing she needed was the father of her children going all gonzo on the most evil men she'd ever had the bad occasion to meet. "I don't want Jace in the canyons anymore."

Ash reached for her hand, rubbed it. "You're scared. Your fingers are trembling."

"I'm not scared for me. I honestly believe I'm too huge to be a target for Wolf. It's going to take a crane to get me off this sofa. My husband is another matter. And Wolf also threatened my uncle and Lu." Sawyer sipped some tea for strength. "I want you to convince Jace not to do his job. He wouldn't be happy with me if he knew I was telling you this." Ash handed her a tissue, which she took gratefully. "Just until I have the babies."

Fiona and Ash looked at her, their eyes huge with concern.

"We can't keep Jace from his job, or the canyons. But I'll talk to Uncle Wolf," Ash said with determination.

Sawyer started. "No!"

Fiona looked at her. "Why would Wolf threaten Storm?"

"Wolf said he'll make me miserable for turning on him," Sawyer said miserably. "He knows I told you about the wire and the spying. He said I should have helped my uncle get him the information he needed. But Wolf doesn't understand that my uncle isn't his pawn. I'm not his pawn. I'm not going to do anything to hurt Jace. I'm a Callahan now."

"That's right," Ash said. "Wolf has never understood that Callahans stick together."

"This is too hard for her to deal with," Fiona said to Ash. "I'll talk to Wolf myself." She stood, a resolute figure in a turquoise-blue dress and delicate white boots. "In fact, I'll kick his mangy a—"

"No, Aunt." Ash pulled Fiona back down next to her. "All Sawyer wants us to do is keep Jace from the firing line. There'll be no butt-kicking. In fact, we're going to lie very low."

Fiona patted Sawyer's hand. "My niece is right. You

just rest and don't think another thing about all this Wolf nonsense."

"Tell me the plan so I can at least enjoy it vicariously."

Ash looked at her. "You're tough, I'll grant you that. But we don't have a plan. Yet. But we will."

Sawyer leaned back. "I knew I could count on you."

"Don't let Wolf rattle you. All sound and fury, but that's it." Fiona got up. "Next time I come by, I'm bringing catalogs for you to peruse for baby decor."

"Thank you, Fiona." Sawyer managed a smile.

"In the meantime, I'm sure my brother told you not to open the door to anyone," Ash said.

"I can't even get up," Sawyer pointed out.

"That's right." Ash looked at her. "How do people get in to see you, like the nurse?"

"I've been leaving the door unlocked, since I'm lying right here." Sawyer didn't mention she'd placed a pink Taser and a can of pepper spray under her floral sofa, within easy reach. The Taser had been a housewarming gift from Lu, the pepper spray from the sheriff's wife. "Jace says the door has to be locked from now on. But Lu and Storm are next door, and the sheriff is right around the corner—"

"Listen to my brother," Ash said. "Sometimes he actually makes sense." There were hugs all around and the two women left.

Sawyer sank against the pillow, closed her eyes and hoped they could keep Jace from canyon duty tonight. She didn't want the father of her children in danger—especially when Wolf had sounded so very definite about what he planned to do to her uncle and her husband.

Wolf had been angry. As if she'd somehow betrayed him. She couldn't figure out why he should feel betrayed.

She'd never been on Team Wolf. She hated him for exactly the same reasons the Callahans did: he was determined to destroy them. She wished she was still fit, could still fight the good fight. Prove herself to Jace.

She must have dozed off, because the babies kicked inside her, waking her—and then the door blew open. She gasped and reached for the Taser.

"Jace! What are you doing here?"

She stared at her husband. He was carrying a bouquet of flowers and a box that looked as if it came from the Books'n'Bingo Society tearoom.

"I was relieved of canyon duty," he said. "Where'd you get the cute little pink equalizer?"

"I'm not supposed to tell, but Lu gave it to me. She said no woman should be without one. Who took your shift?"

He closed the door. "My sister." He raised a brow, handed over the flowers. "She said she wanted me to have a night off with my bride."

"That was nice of her," Sawyer said, feeling a bit guilty.

He leaned over and gave her a big smooch. "That flowery sofa sure looks good with you on it."

"I don't want Ash in the canyons," Sawyer said, ignoring his flattery. It was harder to ignore his strong muscles as he wrapped big hands around her stomach.

"No one tells little sister what to do." He kissed Sawyer's belly. "I hope her namesake doesn't follow that closely in her aunt's footsteps, but I'm afraid she probably will. None of the Callahan females know how to mind."

Sawyer snorted. "Thank you for the flowers. And are those snacks?"

"I was warned that it would be best if I showed up

bearing gifts, although I told my sister that you'd be happy just to see me."

Sawyer raised a brow. "And I am. Hand me a cookie. Can't you send Dante or Tighe to the canyon instead of Ash?" She was trying to keep the matter light, but Wolf had really worried her.

"Everybody's got their own assignments. Ash just relieved me of mine because she didn't need to guard Fiona tonight. Fiona said she was taking Burke to a movie and that she didn't require watching, so Ash kicked me off the grid."

That wasn't the result Sawyer had wanted. She supposed she should have seen that coming, though. "I thought Ash wasn't supposed to be in the canyons alone."

"She's not, really. Galen doesn't like it. But she's earned her stripes. There's really not anything we can do about it." He looked at the Taser. "I hope you never have to use this, but I wish I'd thought of it." He kissed her hand. "More to the point, I wish my wife didn't have to be confined to bed with a Taser because my uncle's such a—"

"Not in front of the babies," Sawyer teased.

"I can watch my mouth. I'll watch yours, too," he said, kissing her, and Sawyer sighed with happiness as Jace wrapped her in his arms.

"So I heard Wolf called you," he said, and Sawyer froze.

"They weren't supposed to tell you!"

He looked at her. "Who wasn't supposed to tell me?"

"Fiona and Ash!"

He raised a brow. "Tell me what?"

She hesitated. "Who told you Wolf called me?"

"Your uncle." Jace frowned at her. "Why wouldn't you want me to know?"

"I just don't. Didn't. And don't frown at me. I've got a lot on my mind and I feel suddenly like I might be prone to tears."

He smiled. "That'd be a first. I've never seen you cry."

She sighed and leaned back, closed her eyes for a minute. "Don't tempt me. I might wail all over you, and I assure you, it won't be pretty."

"Anyway, back to Wolf," he prompted.

"I didn't want you to know because I didn't want you going all ape on his big stupid self. I'd like to keep you alive for the duration of our marriage," she snapped.

"Duration?" He rubbed her belly. "You don't have to protect me from my uncle. Although I realize it's second nature to you. I'm the man, I'll protect my family." He kissed her hand. "And I want to start protecting you by putting the wedding ring I gave you on your hand."

She looked at him. "How will it protect me?"

"It's a magic ring. Didn't I tell you?" He grinned at her, sexy as sin. "Where is it?"

"In my purse. Under the sofa ruffle, next to the Taser and the pepper spray."

"Another gift from Lu?"

"The sheriff's wife."

He grunted as he checked out her stock under the ruffle. "I'm impressed. All you need now are handcuffs and maybe a slingshot."

She sat up. "I hadn't thought of a slingshot!"

"Easy, babe. I wasn't serious." He sighed, and pulled out the ring box. "Now let's get this magic ring on you, so you can lie here and rest in a bubble of good health and happy thoughts."

She put out her finger. "Go for it."

"That easy? You've had the ring this long and suddenly you don't mind wearing it?"

"I want to make you happy," she said softly. "Anyway, I wanted to wear your ring for a long time."

"I know. You won me just for that purpose." He slipped the ring on her finger, looked at it for a minute. "You have beautiful hands. This is exactly how I imagined it would look on them."

She smiled. "That's sweet, Jace."

He kissed her. "It's true. I wanted you to have the most beautiful ring I could find, for my most beautiful bride. I didn't want you to regret breaking your piggy bank wide-open for me."

"You have a lot of ego, cowboy."

He grinned. "I know."

Just when she thought she couldn't be any happier, that maybe everything that had kept them apart was totally in the past now, the door opened with a crash.

Wolf walked in with a nasty, know-it-all grin on his face.

"Hello, nephew, Ms. Cash," he said, and Jace tensed.

"How dare you enter my home without knocking?" Sawyer demanded, incensed. "You go right back out and knock. When I say come in, then you may. Until then, you're not a welcome guest. And it's Mrs. Callahan to you, thanks."

He grinned at her, and her blood boiled. This was exactly why her and Jace's marriage was always in a state of disarray. This man was a certain, surefire disruptor.

Something had to change.

"If you don't go outside and wait to be invited to enter

like a normal person," Sawyer said, "I'll call Sheriff Cartwright."

"Now, young lady," Wolf said, his voice patronizing.

God, she hated being patronized. And she hated being helpless.

She hit him with her Taser, and Wolf collapsed to the floor.

"Nice shot," Jace said.

"He looks like he's drooling a bit. Will you go make sure he doesn't drool on my new rug Fiona got me? I'll call the sheriff."

"Never mind." Jace sighed and sent a text. "The cleanup crew will be here in a minute." He went to check on his uncle, turning him faceup with his boot. "When are you ever going to learn?"

Wolf lay almost deathly still. "I didn't kill him, did I?" Sawyer asked. "I know Running Bear has rules about killing off his prodigal son."

"You didn't kill him. But that little pink version of whoop-ass works much better than I thought it would." Jace looked at her. "What am I going to do with you?"

She just hoped her husband loved her. "I'll let you decide."

He looked out the window. "The cavalry's arrived. They must have been in town." He opened the door, and Galen and Sloan came inside.

"Hello, Sawyer," they said, like respectful schoolboys, and then looked down at their uncle.

"He never learns," Sloan said.

Ash appeared in the doorway. "Toss him in the back of the truck with the rest of the trash we need to haul off."

Galen looked at Sawyer. "Are you all right?"

She nodded. "I'm fine."

"Your work? I presume my brother didn't do this," Galen said, eyeing the pink gun.

"Yes. Thanks."

Galen looked at Jace. "Can I see you outside?" he asked, as Wolf was rolled up in a tarp Ash provided. Their uncle was whisked away, as if he'd never been there.

Jace glanced at his wife. "I'll be right back. You take a nap."

He followed his brother outside. "What's up?"

They watched as Wolf was bundled into the truck bed. "This can't go on," Galen said. "Next time, you might not be here. And my understanding of the situation is that Wolf is really aggravated with the Cashs."

"He was just trying to cause trouble. He saw my truck, and came in, anyway," Jace pointed out. "My wife had issues with his mouth. She doesn't like disrespect."

"She was trying to prove she's on our side."

"I don't know," Jace said. "Maybe." He didn't think Sawyer had time enough to think through the situation. She'd merely reacted. "Anyway, she has nothing to prove. She's a Callahan."

"Ash says Sawyer's all hung up about the fact that she spied for her uncle." Galen shrugged. "I don't want her overcompensating. Wolf's dangerous. So are his compadres. Tell her."

"Tell her what?"

"Tell her everything is good, that she doesn't need to prove herself to you anymore."

"She doesn't."

"Try to understand the feelings in her heart."

Sawyer hadn't wanted to wear his ring before. Maybe Galen had a point. Jace shrugged. "I'll talk to her."

Galen slapped him on the back. "See you at the ranch later for the meeting."

He'd forgotten. He glanced back at the duplex, saw Sawyer's drawn face peering out at them. "I don't know if I can leave, Galen."

His brother nodded, got in his truck. "I understand. Sawyer might feel better if she wasn't alone tonight, anyway, considering Wolf's unexpected visit."

Jace nodded, went inside and closed the door.

"Now what happens?" Sawyer asked.

"Now you and I go back to where we were." He sat next to her for a long, sweet kiss.

"Jace, wait." She pulled back. "You can't just act like nothing happened."

"What do you mean? Nothing did happen. Not really. My uncle was being rude, you taught him a lesson."

"And you're okay with me shooting him?"

"You deserve a blue ribbon. My own Annie Oakley." He put a hand on her stomach. "My uncle got what was coming to him."

She nodded. "Okay."

But he sensed she wasn't. Not really.

"I'm going to nap, if you don't mind."

"No problem. I'll nap with you."

"No, Jace." She shook her head. "I think I want to be alone for a while."

He hesitated. Galen had just postulated that she wouldn't want to be alone after Wolf's visit. She was basically telling him to leave.

"Are you sure?"

"I'm sure."

He had the uncomfortable feeling that they were married, but not really together. Wherever she was, that was his home, too, right? Yet Sawyer was kicking him out, like a date who'd stayed too long. "Guess I'll head over to the family meeting, then. Text me, or call me, if you need anything."

"I'll be fine. I'm just going to sleep."

He kissed her and left, not feeling good about it all. Every single woman who'd had a bad man walk into her home wouldn't want to be alone—every single woman except maybe Ash and Fiona. Jace shook his head. He glanced toward the window, but Sawyer wasn't looking out at him.

He had the uncomfortable feeling something wasn't right, but whatever it might be wasn't penetrating his thick skull. Jace started his truck and headed to Rancho Diablo.

Chapter Thirteen

Sawyer didn't call him to come around much, and Jace had the uncomfortable feeling that his wife had separated emotionally from him in some way. For two months, he was an occasional guest at the duplex, only invited every once and again. He got used to carrying a sleeping bag for the nights his wife allowed him to stay over, which wasn't more than once a week.

Sawyer said she liked being alone, that as uncomfortable as she was with the aches and pains that kept her awake, she didn't want to keep him awake, as well. He supposed that made sense, but he'd rather be with his wife. Besides the sofa, there wasn't a stick of furniture in the house—no bed, no kitchen table, nothing. He'd offered, as had Fiona and Ash, to bring catalogs for her to choose from, but Sawyer shook her head.

She did, however, let Fiona and Ash and Lu bring over two white cribs from the ranch, and all the baby things their hearts desired for the nursery. He wasn't sure what to think about that. Apparently Sawyer planned on staying in the little duplex, but she couldn't sleep on the floral sofa forever.

He was stuck in serious limbo.

And then in late April he got the call from Storm, of

all people, that they'd taken Sawyer to the hospital. Jace was about to tear out of the meeting that was being held in the upstairs library, where his brothers and sister were arguing about what might have happened to the Diablo mustangs, which hadn't been seen in months, when Storm said, "And by the way, Sawyer says not to come until she calls you."

"What?" He'd just about had it with all the stop signs from his darling wife.

"She says she's just gone into labor. Could be hours before she has the babies. She wants you to keep working—in fact, she said she expects you to understand that you're going to have your fair share of diaper and bottle duty soon, so put your time in at the ranch now, while you can."

Jace frowned. That sounded a little better. "I'm coming, anyway."

"I thought you'd feel that way," Storm said cheerfully. "If you wouldn't mind, bring a thermos of coffee, would you? This stuff here is dreck. If we're going to be here for a long time, I think you're going to want something that resembles coffee and not sludge."

"Sure. Thanks, Storm." He hung up, and his family looked at him.

"Babies are on the way." As he said it, his chest filled with pride.

"It's time! I'm going to be an aunt again!" Ash leaped from the sofa and hugged his neck. "I'll drive you. Come on."

He stared around the room at his brothers, who grinned at him with knowing expressions.

"It's your turn," Sloan said. "You don't know it, but your life is about to change. It'll never be the same again.

Enjoy these last few moments of rarified pre-daddy air, because you'll never know them again for the rest of your life. What you're about to smell is entirely different."

His brothers guffawed like asses.

"No sleep. No silence," Dante said. "No more navel gazing, which you have to admit, you've honed to a fine art."

Jace raised a brow.

Tighe leaned back on the sofa with a grin. "From now on, no such thing as life unplanned. Every moment has a schedule, a routine. You'll feel guilty if you're not at ballet lessons, church groups, or being ridden like a pony."

His brothers didn't seem to be too unhappy. Rather, they seemed like men who lived in a secret world he had yet to enter. "Anything else?"

Falcon waved a majestic hand. "We have no more secrets to offer. You're in the daddy club now. Just be sure you remember that every day that ends in *y* now starts with baby and ends with baby." He grinned, proud of his contribution.

"What a bunch of wienies," Ash said. "Are you trying to scare him to death?"

"For me it's the scrapbooking," Galen said. "The photo puzzles, the picture files. How to capture all the little moments that don't seem important to anyone else but you. Like the first time they smile at you." He grinned at Jace. "And the first giggle—there's nothing, nothing, nothing better than baby laughter. It's innocent, it's delightful, it's free. And your whole spirit goes straight up like a lightning rod. It's the gift of the Creator, allowing you another peek at true happiness."

They all stared at Galen.

"Wow," Ash said, "you almost made me want to have a baby, Galen."

Jace's throat went tight. Everything his brothers teased him about sounded awesome. He couldn't wait to meet his own children, to hold them. He was a family man, through and through. "I can't wait," he said, past the tightness.

His brothers came over and pounded his back.

"Congratulations, bro," Sloan said. "We tease, but only because we know you wanted it from the time you were a kid. Family was always your cause."

His other brothers murmured in agreement.

"Thanks," Ash said. "He says thanks. He has to go now, as he's having my niece and nephew. Goodbye, brothers. Try to achieve world peace while we're gone, okay? Find the Diablos, and other creative things. In other words, be productive."

She pulled Jace down the hall, and he let her. "Gosh, they're windbags," she said. "I love them, but holy smoke. Always have to stick their scrawny little oars in. Are you all right?"

"Yeah. I promised Storm a thermos of coffee. He says the coffee there isn't up to par."

"I'll do it. You go change, and I'll fill up some thermoses and grab some snacks. Might be a long wait. None of us have delivered in under eight hours, I don't think."

"Us?" he teased.

"We Callahans. You're having the last children of the family, Jace, unless the talking heads upstairs become more focused on babymaking. Go change those clothes. You've been riding canyon, and you don't want to insult your new babies' nostrils with eau de barn."

"Ash, you'll have children," Jace said, feeling as if he

needed to comfort his sister. She had such a broken heart over Xav Phillips. But there was nothing that could be done about it. "You'll find the right man one day, and you'll have a baby."

"Go," she said, waving a thermos at him. "Today is your day. And if you stand around yakking like the rest of our brothers, we'll miss the arrival of my niece and nephew. One thing your little ones are going to always know is that their aunt Ash was right there with a catcher's mitt, waiting to teach them the ways."

He loved his sister. More than anyone, she had his back. She was tough and fearless, and he wished he was better at making the women in his life happy.

But what Ash said made sense. He, too, was going to be there, from the beginning. When they fell, when they succeeded, his children were always going to know that their father loved them.

Even if their mother wasn't in love with him.

He tore up the stairs, his mind in overdrive. He showered, so fast it couldn't be called a shower but a rinse, then jumped into fresh jeans, grabbed a clean shirt. Hauled down the stairs when Ash roared up at him that he was slower than molasses at Christmas, and that the babies were going to be going off to college before he pulled his head out. By his watch, he'd been upstairs all of eight minutes.

He hurried through the house and followed his sister out the door. "Let me carry the picnic," he said, taking the hamper from her. "What'd you pack? Enough food for the entire hospital?"

"The nursing staff will want cookies. It's manners to share what you have with nurses and visitors. Everybody likes a party, Jace, and we want the babies spoiled by all. They've had a tough start."

"But they're not going to be eating the cookies," he said, laughing.

"You laugh, brother, but when you share your toys, other people like you."

He held the door so she could hop in the truck. Then he shoved the hamper in the back and went around to the driver's side, thinking about sharing his toys. They hadn't really had toys to speak of in the tribe, but his Callahan nieces and nephews had toys like mad, and maybe he should stop by the hospital gift shop to pick up bears....

Just then a sting in his chest stopped his thoughts. Jace felt himself falling back from the truck door he'd been about to open, and it was so very strange to be falling, not in control of himself, staring up at the sky, with Ash's wide eyes staring down at him. Jace was amazed that he couldn't feel his body. He was floating, and felt strange, like he'd never felt before, light and airy, his mind no longer full of a thousand thoughts.

The last thing he remembered was Ash's frantic screams. He wanted to tell her it was going to be all right, that he'd protect her; he always had, he always would. He'd take care of Sawyer and the babies, too, because that's what he did. He was a guard against darkness and evil, a shield for the good in the world, because Running Bear had told him from the time he was young that he was a warrior.

But he was so tired. So he went to sleep, overtaken by exhaustion, but comforted by the thought that when he woke up he was going to tell his wife how much he loved her.

Sawyer was his whole life.

"JACE CAN COME in now," Sawyer told her uncle and Lu. She'd had an emergency C-section, and the babies were doing well, though they were tiny. Sawyer thought Ashley and Jason were the most beautiful babies she'd ever seen, and before she fell asleep, she wanted to see the expression on Jace's face when he was introduced to his children.

He was going to be so proud.

Ash wore a funny look. "Jace will be by in a little while."

Sawyer thought he'd have been breaking down the door by now. In fact, she was amazed that Jace had waited so patiently until after she'd had the C-section to come barreling in. She hadn't wanted him to worry as she had when the doctor had told her they'd have to perform the emergency procedure. The babies had been stressed, and everything had moved awfully fast.

"Where is he?" she asked Ash.

His sister set two adorable teddy bears down in the window. "He got called to do something at the ranch. It couldn't be avoided."

Ash was acting strange. She'd been tickled and joyful when she'd seen the babies, snapping a thousand pictures—but when the newborns were whisked away to the neonatal nursery, she'd turned solemn. Sawyer thought her sister-in-law's eyes were red, as if she'd been crying.

That was impossible. Ash never cried.

"Are you all right, Ash?"

"Me? I'm fine. Good job bringing my namesake into the world."

Sawyer smiled. "It was an amazing experience. I can't wait to do it again someday."

Ash looked pained. "You should sleep now. What do

they feed you around here, anyhow? I brought a hamper of goodies to Lu and Storm and the staff. You want me to sneak you something?"

She shook her head, lay back against the pillow. "No, thanks. I'll just wait for Jace to get here. I think the nurses do some special candlelight dinner thing for the mom and dad after the babies are born."

Ash hesitated. "Tonight?"

"I think the night of the birth, yes. But I'm sure it could be another night, too. I'll go home the day after tomorrow, though the babies will stay a little longer. Why?"

"No reason."

Sawyer studied Ash, checking out her pale face and her eyes, which didn't seem quite as bubbly as they had when she'd visited her at the duplex. And Ash had been a frequent visitor. Almost daily. Like a bodyguard.

They were all bodyguards and protectors, Sawyer included. Jace was, too—and he wouldn't have missed the babies' birth for anything. He would have torn a hole in the wall to get to his kids, if for no other reason than to see for himself that they were all right, that they had everything they needed. The warrior code was strong in Jace. He was more quiet about it than some of the other brothers, and even Ash—but he was a strong defender.

And he would have been here for his children.

"Where is he?" she demanded. "And don't tell me he's doing something at the ranch, because your face is giving you away. You look like a ghost has infested your grave."

Ash burst into tears. "I can't tell you."

Alarm flooded Sawyer's bloodstream. "You'd better tell me, or I'll get out of this bed and pull your hair."

Ash blew her nose, tears brimming in her eyes. "I want to tell you, but I can't."

Sawyer made a move to get up, which hurt like hell because her stitches pulled, and Ash gasped, put her hands up in surrender.

"Get back in the damn bed! If the nurses see you moving around, they'll yell at me."

"Since when do you care who's yelling at you about what? Where's Jace?"

"In the operating room," Ash said. "He had a slight accident."

Sawyer blinked. "It's not slight if he's in the O.R." Her heart rate sped up uncomfortably.

"He's going to be fine." Ash swallowed hard, blew her nose on a tissue. "But I have to go now, Sawyer."

"If you step one foot out that door, I'm changing Ashley's name to Bessie Brunhilda Callahan—"

"You wouldn't!"

"I would. And you'll no longer be the namesake aunt," Sawyer said coldly. "Tell me everything about my husband."

Ash stalked around the room, upset. "We were on our way here. He'd just put the hamper in the truck when—" her eyes widened as she looked at Sawyer "—when someone shot him."

Sawyer gasped. "Shot him!"

"Don't worry. The doctors wasted no time getting him into the O.R. And Galen's in there overseeing everything, and no doubt whispering the words of healing to him."

"I've got to see him!" Sawyer wished she could get out of this stupid bed. She was tired of being helpless. "Find a nurse who will wheel me to his room."

"No nurse will. There's not a one who will risk her job, so you can forget that. And don't ask me, I'm already in enough trouble." Ash was clearly miserable. "I shouldn't have even told you. Your uncle Storm told me not to. I thought that was good advice. But I'm so worried that I blabbed!" she said with a wail. "I never blab!"

Ash was so upset about her brother that she wasn't herself. Sawyer tried to stay calm despite the panic swamping her. "He'll be all right, won't he? Where'd he get shot?"

"The bullet hit a lung," Ash said, sobbing into a tissue. "I'm so sorry. I shouldn't have told you. I should have listened to your uncle." She blew her nose again, wiped her eyes, and Sawyer felt herself grow cold inside. Tight and angry. Someone had shot her husband, had tried to take away the father of her children. Whoever it was had meant business, aiming, no doubt, for his heart.

Wolf had meant to kill his nephew. Wolf, or perhaps one of his minions, had done his best to steal away what she wanted more than anything on this earth.

She'd shot Wolf with the Taser, and he'd returned the favor.

"I'm going to kill him," she muttered under her breath, and Ash straightened at her furious words.

"You'll have to beat me to it," she said softly, and Sawyer's skin crawled at her tone. "I don't care what Running Bear says. It's my life's mission to make sure my uncle never tries to hurt any of my family ever again."

Chapter Fourteen

Jace awakened, feeling like death. He was groggy, he hurt like hell and something wasn't right with his body. It was out of focus in some strange way. And he wasn't at home. Something had happened to him. He was going to be with his babies at their births, and then he'd fallen. He remembered that much, because of the deep beauty of the sky overhead and Ash's face hovering over him, her navy eyes wide with fear. That's what was wrong— Ash was never afraid.

His sister had been terrified.

"You awake?" he heard someone ask.

He peered at the corner of the room. "Where am I?" he asked.

"In the hospital," the soothing voice replied.

He knew that voice. It spoke to his soul, reminded him of who he was. "Grandfather. What happened?"

"You were shot." Running Bear stepped closer to the bed to look down at him. "Coming from the north, where the canyons are, three scouts crossed Rancho Diablo. One of them shot you."

It made sense. "Don't worry. I've been shot before, when I was in... When I was somewhere."

"You were overseas," Running Bear murmured. "In Iraq. But the enemy here meant to kill you, too."

"Why?"

"My son is evil. There is no purpose to his desire to kill. His heart is black, and it can never be clean again. He has forgotten the old ways, his ancestors, the ancient words, loyalty to family. Everything has left him. So you must live."

Jace grunted, but it came out more like a pained groan. "Of course I'm going to live. I survived Iraq. I can survive my uncle."

His grandfather touched Jace's forehead, put a hand over his heart, and Jace felt strength flood into him.

"Energy transfer," Running Bear said. "Rest. Galen was in the O.R. with you. He spoke the healing words. You will live to fight another day."

"I'll live to fight many years." He looked up at his grandfather. "I have babies to teach the ways to. Where are my children? Where's Sawyer?"

"One floor down. You'll see her soon."

"I'll see her now." He struggled to sit up, but his grandfather pushed him gently back into the bed.

"I've got to go," Jace said. "Sawyer needs to know that I'm all right. I'm going to take care of her and protect her always."

"She knows." Running Bear's hand pressed against him. "You can't take danger to her."

Jace stared at him. "What do you mean?"

"You now walk with a shadow. It's not safe to go there."

A chill sliced into Jace. "Am I the one you spoke of, the hunted one?" he asked desperately. "The one who'll bring devastation and danger to the family?"

One of the seven Callahan siblings was the hunted one, but he'd never thought it was him. Jace had always been the family man, the one who longed for tribe, for community, for his own to hold. "Am I?" he demanded.

"I don't know," Running Bear said. "I only know the mysteries, not who puts them in motion."

"It's not me." Jace again tried to make it to the edge of the bed. "It's *not* me. And I have to be with Sawyer. She's my heart, my life, Grandfather."

"I know. But don't take danger to her door."

"How?" He looked at the chief impatiently. "Are they here? Will they try to kill me again? Even here?"

Running Bear sighed. "I do not know the answers."

"You didn't know I was going to be shot, either."

"I did not. Evil hides itself in many forms. Where my son is concerned, I do not always see." His dark eyes looked deeply sad.

He put a hand in front of Jace's face briefly. "Now sleep," he told him. "Sleep and heal. You were born a warrior. You are a shepherd to the land and your family. Sleep, and let healing chase away the evil."

Jace was about to tell his grandfather that he was sorry, he had to get to his wife and babies no matter what—but then he was overcome by weariness so profound that he fell back into the hospital bed, worn-out.

And then peace claimed him. He dreamed of the Diablos running through the canyons, wild and free. He rode a Diablo, and his children rode with him, and his heart was alive and shining with the mysticism and beauty of the spirits. Sawyer stood on a mesa far away, watching proudly. It was a dark, mystical dream, infused with wonder and breathtaking splendor, and Jace was content to watch from afar, called by the majesty, resting in the knowledge that Sawyer and his children were in good hands.

And while he watched himself riding with his children, he heard his grandfather's voice in the background, murmuring the ancient words without pause. Jace heard soft music from a flute that played the lullabies he'd heard in the tribe, as his grandfather's voice reminded him of the spirits.

He was hypnotized and calm, and safe.

For now.

SALLY CLAUSEN CAME to check on Sawyer, and Sawyer realized the nurse was exactly the visitor she needed. "I have to see my husband."

"You will soon," Sally said. "For now it's important that you rest. Your body's been through a lot."

"Sally, help me get to my husband," Sawyer begged. "If I leave here with anyone but a nurse, I'll get put right back in my bed. I know you can spring me. Wheel me to the nursery so I can see my children, and then slip me into my husband's room. Please."

"I can't." Sally's eyes were huge with concern. "Sawyer, I'd do anything for you, but there's a guard on your husband's door in the ICU. No one's getting in except the chief."

"Chief Running Bear?"

"Yes." The nurse nodded. "He's not really supposed to be in there, but he's in a trance or something. No one dares disturb him, especially not since Jace is doing so much better. It was really touch and go for a while."

Sally's eyes widened further at Sawyer's gasp.

"I think I've said too much already," the nurse stated.

"Look, you rest, Sawyer. You want to be strong when your husband is ready to wake up, don't you?"

"Wake up?" Sawyer glared at her. "What do you mean, wake up?"

Sally sighed. "He's in a slight coma."

"It is either a coma or it's not." Her blood roared in her ears. "You go out there and you find the chief of staff of this hospital, and you tell him that I want to see my husband. Today."

Sally backed up at Sawyer's ferocity. "I'll tell the head nurse and she'll pass the word along. But I doubt they'll let you. It's important that Jace rest. Even Ash can't get in to see him."

"Oh, Ash will find a way. Nothing keeps Ash from her brothers, trust me on that." Sawyer slumped back in the bed. "Fine. You pass my message along to the chief of staff. And I'm sorry I crabbed on you, Sally. You've been a really good friend, and I'm…"

"Just feeling at your wits' end. I know. I would be, too. Get some rest." She went out the door, her cheerful sunniness restored, and Sawyer told herself she wasn't going to have any friends left if she didn't quit snapping at everyone who came into her room. She was just so afraid for Jace! "I should have aimed for Wolf's heart with that Taser," she muttered crankily. "Maybe I could have short-circuited it since it's such a tiny, black piece of evil."

She was stunned when Running Bear walked into the room, his dark face lined with exhaustion. "Running Bear!"

"Hello, Sawyer."

She'd never seen the chief look so tired. "There's Rancho Diablo coffee in that thermos, and cookies in the tin. Fiona brings by a truckload of stuff every day, she says to bribe the nursing staff to take good care of her Callahans. Please, help yourself. I'm pretty sure you need Fiona's sugar jump."

It was a well-known fact that the chief had a sweet tooth for Fiona's baking, not that it showed on his lean frame.

"Your babies are strong," he said.

Sawyer smiled. "Small, but very strong, according to the doctors."

"They have mighty spirits. Their bodies will grow and they will gain weight. All will be well." He munched on a cookie, his color returning a bit. "You have a strong spirit, too."

"I don't think I do," Sawyer said. "I'm so scared, I feel weak."

"Jace is fine. You will see."

She looked at the chief. "I thought he was in a coma."

"He will awaken because he lives for you."

Their marriage hadn't exactly been a bedrock of marital bliss. "I don't know if he'd agree."

"Jace is strong because of you, and you're strong because of him. That can't be broken, unless one of you chooses it."

Was that a warning or just a bland statement? "What can I do to help him? They won't let me see him."

"You will tonight. When you do, tell him what you've been wanting to tell him for a long time."

She looked at Running Bear. "I will."

"It will help him to hear the words. Tell him, too, about his children. That will give him the will to heal faster."

"I'll gladly do it, Running Bear." Time had seemed to be moving so quickly for her and Jace, and she'd never really felt comfortable falling for him. As if she'd somehow taken advantage of the Callahan family. She'd felt awkward because of why she'd hired on at Rancho Diablo—but always, always, she'd loved Jace.

"We understand loyalty in our family," Running Bear said. "Do not be afraid that you are loyal. You would not be right for Jace if you were not true to your family."

"Thank you," she murmured. "How will I see him tonight? No one will take me."

"Jace needs his family. He always has. It's from family that he draws his strength." Running Bear left the room as silently as he'd walked in, and Sawyer sank back against the pillow.

She had to devise a plot to get to her husband. Tomorrow she'd be released, so she'd be free then. She could visit the babies as she liked, too. But the sooner Jace got well, the sooner they could all be together.

Running Bear said Jace was strong because of her. If that was true, then he needed her now.

She got up, pain shooting through her abdomen.

Fiona announced herself just then in a flurry of pink, the scent of warm cinnamon surrounding her like a cloud. "Hello, Sawyer!"

Sawyer grabbed a pair of sandals she'd planned to wear home. "Hi, Fiona."

"What are you doing?" She came over to help with the sandals so Sawyer wouldn't pull the stitches in her stomach.

"Going to see Jace."

"Oh," his aunt said mildly. "I happened to note that the nursing staff at the desk seem to be a bit preoccupied."

"You just happened to notice that?" Sawyer asked, knowing Fiona loved to meddle.

"I'm a very observant person." She shrugged. "And Running Bear told me you might need some help."

"He thinks my place is with Jace."

"Exactly! The two of you need a total restart, in my opinion. No more of this halfway-married business."

"Halfway married?"

"Indeed. The two of you don't live together. If I hadn't seen your check from the ball, and cashed it, I wouldn't have believed you were the woman who bid so hard for my nephew."

"Fiona, do you have something on your mind?" Sawyer asked, a bit startled by the unusual amount of opinions the woman was sharing.

"Is there ever a time I don't?"

She sat on the bed. "Feel free to share it. But hurry. I'm on a mission." Sawyer waited, her gaze on the tiny woman who ran Rancho Diablo.

"My nephew was shot, I believe, because Wolf is angry that Jace married you. You were supposed to be Wolf's ace in the hole, and as you know, aces are very important."

Sawyer swallowed hard against the guilt rising inside her. "He did say he'd make me regret turning on him. Those were his words."

"But you were never on his side."

"No. I wasn't."

"You must make Wolf believe you have seen the error of your ways."

Sawyer stared at the determined woman who was the backbone for Diablo. "All I care about is my husband and my children. Whatever Wolf thinks is immaterial. He can take a flying leap. And if I were he, I'd be watching my back. I believe he may have a Callahan after him who's not easily intimidated."

Fiona shook her head. "For Jace's sake, for your children's sake, you may have to appear to be more Team Wolf than Team Callahan for the time being."

"I won't do it."

"Not even if it calms Wolf down? Keeps him from sending more agents after your husband? Or your children?" Fiona looked at her curiously. "Then what's your plan?"

"My plan right now is to sneak down the hall to see my husband. When my babies are stronger and the hospital says they can be released, when my husband is well enough, I'm taking him home. We're going to be a family. And I don't care what Wolf thinks about that. I can protect my own family."

"All a very fine plan, except that you can't expect Jace to live holed up in that tiny duplex with you. He belongs at Rancho Diablo."

"It may be months before he's healed. Jace is off *your* team for now." Fiona didn't understand. Sawyer was going to do whatever she had to do to keep her family safe—and if that meant moving to the ends of the earth, that's what they'd do. "Jace already said we should go into hiding. He took me to Colorado for that purpose." She walked to the door of the hospital room. "Running Bear specifically said at that time that we should be in hiding. I should have listened to his very wise advice. Now," she said, holding Fiona in front of her, "walk slowly past the nurses' station, but not too slowly, because you're always a whirlwind. But I can't keep up with you if you walk your normal flying-aunt gait."

"What are you going to do?"

"I'm taking a walk down the hall with my dear one-time employer," Sawyer said, "which is good, because the nurses advised me to walk a little."

"A little," Fiona said. "Not to the ICU to see your husband."

"Just walk, Fiona."

The older woman sighed. "I don't like being a part of a plot."

"You love being part of a plot. Keep that cheery smile on your face as we stroll to the nursery window so I can see my babies."

"That's better," Fiona said, perking up and not looking so worried. "We can just stand here and look at Jason and Ashley and think about planning their christenings. I'm thinking matching gowns—"

"Continuing on," Sawyer said, as they stopped in front of the nursery window. She took a deep breath at the sight of her children sleeping peacefully, watched over by nurses, and then took Fiona's arm again. "You're doing this for Jace. Keep walking, please."

Fiona sighed, pressed the elevator button. "I've done a lot over the years for my nephews and niece. Twelve nephews and one niece I have, and I don't think any of them ever involved me in a shenanigan like this."

"First time for everything. And I really appreciate you helping me out. I'm desperate to see my husband." They stopped outside Jace's room. "Don't desert me, please."

"I should think not! Make it snappy!" Fiona glanced around the hall. "I'll have you know the Callahans put a wing on this hospital, and have flooded it with Christmas charity ball funds over the years. I'm an honorary chairman of some such. I can't be seen disobeying hospital protocols and orders. Just lay eyes on him and get out!"

The guard who was parked outside the door straightened when he saw Fiona, obviously recognizing her. Then ever so slowly, he turned his head away, a signal that he didn't see them enter Jace's room.

"Cookies for you and a bonus at Christmas. You have my thanks for keeping an eye on one of my favorite nephews. Of course, they're all my favorite, but you understand," Fiona muttered to the guard, and Sawyer hurried inside the room, stunned by the sight of her husband lying so still. She'd never seen Jace motionless like this, almost lifeless. Even when they slept together, he seemed to have one eye open for danger—or on her.

"Jace," she murmured, and his eyes opened.

He didn't speak. She crept closer to the bed.

"Jace, I'm so sorry. I know you got shot because of me." She bent close to him, kissed him on the lips. "Running Bear says I make you strong. If that's true, then just know that I'm here."

He closed his eyes. She wasn't sure he'd even heard her.

"Sawyer, come on!" Fiona said, whispering urgently into the room.

She held Jace's hand, put her head down on his shoulder. He lay on his side, probably because of the location of the shot he'd taken, and Sawyer's heart bled. "Winning you was the best thing I ever did for myself," she softly said, hoping he could hear her, "although probably not the best thing for you."

"Sawyer!" Fiona called. "You're about to be off my cookie list if you don't come on!"

"I have to go," she told her husband, kissing him again. "But you have to see our babies, Jace. They're worth every penny I paid for you," she said, meaning to be lighthearted, bring a little laughter to him in whatever dark place he was in. But she choked on the words. "From now on, it's you and me and the babies. That's our Team Callahan."

She hated to leave him. Reluctantly, she released his hand and left the room. "Thank you," she murmured to the guard, and let Fiona grab her hand to lead her away.

Fiona's eyes were wide with apprehension. "Did he say anything?"

"No." They made their way back past the nurses' station, Sawyer walking as close to Fiona as she could in order to not attract attention. Her heart was melting inside her. "I'm not sure he heard me."

Fiona made a murmur of distress. Sawyer felt suddenly weak, exhausted, and clutched the other woman's arm.

"Don't you dare fall," Fiona said sternly. "I'll never forgive you if you faint right here, when I told you this was a bad idea! You just lean on me and keep putting one foot in front of the other, young lady!"

Jace's aunt was in drill sergeant mode. Her starchiness made Sawyer smile—and keep moving. When they made it back to her room, Sawyer gratefully returned to her bed, and Fiona collapsed into a chair.

"I'm not so sure that little adventure didn't give me an attack of angina!" Fiona said dramatically, with a hand on her chest.

"Have you ever had an angina attack?" Sawyer asked, easing her sandals off with her toes and letting them fall to the floor.

"Goodness, no. Heartburn, yes." Fiona sighed. "You remind me of me when I was your age. Did I ever tell you the story of the magic wedding dress and how it came to be in my possession?"

"No." Sawyer looked at her through half-closed eyes. "I haven't had the pleasure of hearing that tale from your grand collection of fairy tales."

Fiona sniffed. "I detect a bit of irony in your voice."

"Respect, more likely."

"Glad to hear it. Because after what you just put me through, you and I are going to have a serious discussion about the fact that the magic wedding dress hasn't been aired out in quite a while."

"Why tell me?" Sawyer asked. "Ash is the one you should be spinning tales to."

"Because," Fiona said, "you're the one whose marriage requires a complete makeover, as I said before. You married Jace under false pretenses, knowing all the while you were spying on our family for your uncle." She waved a hand at Sawyer's glare. "Don't deny it. And the only way to make such a deception right is to wear the magic wedding dress and start the whole thing over. If you're sincere about loving my nephew, and I'm sure you believe that you are."

"What does that mean?" Sawyer demanded.

"Could be baby blues talking. Could be your sense of responsibility, because you don't listen to anyone. You wouldn't go into hiding, as Running Bear recommended. You wouldn't move somewhere safe. You shouldn't have visited Jace today, but you did, even though he's not supposed to have visitors."

"Running Bear told me I'd see him tonight."

"That's right." Fiona nodded. "But it wasn't for you to take into your own hands."

Sawyer sighed. "You're right."

"Of course I am." She nodded again, vigorously. "And I'm right about you getting married again—only this time, you have to do it for the correct reasons. In other words, it's high time you proved yourself as something other than a double agent who accidentally got pregnant in the line of duty."

"I most certainly didn't get pregnant on purpose," Sawyer said hotly.

"Oh, I know. And yet I believe there aren't any true accidents. Remember the night you and Somer were shooting at each other at the Carstairs place in Tempest?"

"I wouldn't have ever tried to harm my cousin! Galen hired me for that job, and I would have protected Rose and her babies with my life!" Sawyer was devastated that the Callahans might think differently.

"I know," Fiona said gently, "but the fact remains that you have some growing to do. I know you're an independent lass—that's why you remind me of myself, and my stubborn Irish roots. But we all have to change, Sawyer, do what's best, even if it's counter to our natures."

"And getting married again does that?" she asked skeptically.

"I'd wait until my nephew is himself once more to find out if he wants to marry you again."

Fear jumped inside Sawyer. "Jace wouldn't change his mind."

"No. He wouldn't want to not be married to you. He has two beautiful babies with you. But," Fiona said, her eyes focused on Sawyer, "he nearly died. Who knows?"

"Running Bear says I make Jace strong," Sawyer said, needing to believe that she was good for her husband.

"Of course you do. And you made him weak, vulnerable. You've kept him at arm's length your entire marriage. He's been sleeping in a sleeping bag, when you'd let him come around the duplex." Fiona stood. "Running Bear is right, he always is. I'd have listened to his first advice, I'd listen to his advice today, and I'd listen to the next advice he gives you, should you ever be so fortunate to be on the receiving end of his wisdom again. Now," Fiona said brightly, "I'm off to the Books'n'Bingo Society to see my friends Mavis Night, Corinne Abernathy and Nadine Waters. We're planning the Christmas ball for next year—and guess who's going to be the final Callahan on the block?"

"Ash. But that didn't go over too well last Christmas, did it? Didn't Ash have a secret bidder she hired to put in a top bid?"

Fiona gave her a wise look. "That's the rumor. But Ash says she didn't rig her own bid. No one knows the identity of the bidder who won her this past year except me. This year, I'm planning to flush that bidder out of the shadows." Fiona grinned. "It's fun chasing bidders out of the shadows. I fully anticipate this particular one will be as productive to our family as the last one was!"

She waved at Sawyer as she left. Sawyer lay back exhausted, her mind in turmoil. She needed to feed her babies, needed to think about everything she'd learned. And she was so overwhelmed by remembering how still Jace had been in his bed that she just wanted to cry.

It was several hours before she remembered Fiona's glee about flushing bidders out of the shadows—and realized the most recent one she'd flushed out had been Sawyer herself, this past Christmas, with the full contents of her savings account.

Fiona had known all along that she was crazy about Jace. She'd also known Sawyer had a conflict of interest where her uncle was concerned. There had been a lot of beautiful women at the ball that night who were just as eager as she was to win Jace.

But Sawyer had been top bidder.

Every word Fiona had said was true. She hadn't acted like a woman who'd won the man of her dreams. Had she felt she hadn't deserved Jace, after all?

She waited until the night shift came on, and her room finally darkened by the nurse. When it sounded quiet in the hall, she slipped on her sandals, and shortly after that Running Bear came to her room, as somehow she'd known he would.

"You have seen Jace," the chief murmured.

"Yes, I have. I'm not sure he knew me, Running Bear."

He nodded. "He did. But he doubts what he knows."

Her heart nearly stopped. "Jace is going to be all right, isn't he?"

Running Bear didn't answer. "You must leave Diablo. When the hospital says you may go, you must take the children and go away."

She gasped. "Go into hiding?"

He looked at her. "Would you have him in further danger?"

"No. Of course not. Nor the children!"

"Then that is what you will do."

Sawyer hesitated. "Fiona thinks Wolf shot my husband because he felt I'd betrayed him. I was supposed to get information for him, through my uncle, apparently. And since I didn't do that, because I married a Callahan instead, this is the price I'm going to have to pay."

Running Bear's expression was inscrutable. "One never tries to discern the mind of someone who does not think with wisdom and understanding. What is known is that Wolf nearly killed Jace."

Sawyer felt herself grow weak with fear. She told herself to not give in to the gnawing panic thundering in her ears. "So you want us to go."

"You and the children. Yes."

"And Jace?"

"Only time will tell."

Running Bear left. Sawyer got back in bed and made herself close her eyes.

Pictures of Jace danced in her head, including the many times he'd made love to her, in the open, wherever, before they'd ever had a bed. Stolen moments she'd known weren't really hers to steal. He was a Callahan, the man she'd fallen for despite knowing that a Callahan would probably never marry a Cash. Couldn't marry a Cash.

She'd set her heart on the moon, and hoped somehow it would come back down to earth, wherever Jace was. She'd gone away for many months, trying to keep her head together about her feelings for him—and still, when she came back, they'd found each other.

They'd made two adorable babies.

But there was a price to pay for love that was stolen.

Chapter Fifteen

Jace opened his eyes to find his worried sister staring at him, almost as if she was looking into his brain through his pupils. "Ash, please take yourself out of my face."

"Oh, Jace!" She flung herself against his chest, and then sat up. "God, I'm sorry! Did I hurt you?"

"No. Of course not. Don't be weird. Where am I?" He glanced around, mystified.

"You're in the hospital," she answered.

"I can see that," he said, feeling a bit crusty. "I mean, where am I? What happened?"

"You're in Diablo," Ash said carefully, as if he was a bit thick, "and you had a small incident. But now you're much better!"

She was too bright and cheerful all of a sudden, when a moment ago she'd been trying to peer inside his skull, her pixie face tight with concern. "So what was this accident?"

"You and I were on the way to the hospital to see the babies and Sawyer. Oh, they're so cute, Jace, so very precious!" His sister perked up considerably. "Little Ashley's going to be just like me when she grows up." Ash leaned close. "I can already tell she has a strong personality. Her aura is very powerful. And I think she may have the wisdom."

He sighed. "How long have I been here?"

She looked confused. "Four days. Don't you want to hear about Jason? And Sawyer?"

Jace sat up. "Yes, I do. And what I also want is out of here. Can you do that for me? Call our brothers for an extract."

Ash shook her head. "I can't do that. The doctors won't release you."

"I'm releasing myself." He went to get out of the bed, was startled by the grogginess that washed over him.

"Whoa, brother." Ash put a hand on his chest, pressing him backward. "Let's not be hasty."

"I want out."

"You don't get everything you want. Don't be a baby."

He snorted. "There's nothing wrong with me. No reason at all why I can't go home."

"You nearly died, Jace. You'll be moved out of ICU today, but I have a feeling it'll be a good few days before you're released."

"What happened?" he asked, disturbed that he couldn't remember.

"You had babies," Ash said. "You and Sawyer had two precious babies. Don't you want to hear about Jason? Sawyer named him after you, you know. Ashley's my namesake, and—"

"Ash," he said, interrupting her, "I don't want to talk about babies."

"Your babies," she said, and he nodded.

"That's right. I don't want to hear about my babies."

"What's the matter with you?" she demanded. "The

babies were practically all you talked about for the past two months."

"Yeah, well. I'm just not ready right now, is all."

Ash blinked. Got up and paced a few steps. Turned to face him. "Sawyer wants to go," she said.

"Probably a good idea."

"You mean that?"

He shrugged. "Yeah. Ash, look. I already know all this. Everything is fine. I saw it in a dream."

"Saw it in a dream? Saw what?"

"Sawyer. The babies. It's all coming back to me now. We were riding the Diablos. Sawyer wasn't—she was watching us from atop a cliff. We were all together. It's fine. I just need to get out of here."

"You and the children were riding, and Sawyer was atop a cliff watching you?" Ash asked curiously, sounding startled.

"Yes. That was the dream." He wasn't certain why his sister looked so strange. It was his dream, nothing that mattered to anyone else.

"But the Diablos haven't been around in months," she murmured.

"I know. I think Wolf's done something to them. I believe the tunnels were a way for the cartel to begin to infiltrate from Loco Diablo—"

"Sister Wind Ranch."

"—to our ranch. That was their plan, to conquer us from below. Really smart plan, too. But Wolf wants the wealth of Rancho Diablo. And the Diablos are the true wealth."

"He doesn't know that," Ash said, her voice full of passion. "Wolf doesn't understand the spirits, or the ways."

Jace considered that. His brain was foggy; every fiber

of his body seemed to be drifting. Maybe it was the medication messing with him.

"None of this matters, Jace. What matters is you and Sawyer and your family."

He knew that. Deep inside him, he knew it. But he also knew that the shot that had hit him could just as easily have been intended for Sawyer—or his children. Sawyer had stunned Wolf with her Taser—and Wolf had been looking for revenge, a reminder that he called the shots. Had he ordered that Jace be killed, or just badly wounded? It didn't matter, because whatever the intention, he'd nearly died. If that same shot had been aimed at Sawyer, it might have killed her, and that would devastate him. He wasn't certain he could survive something happening to his wife. Whatever else had gone on between them, Sawyer was the only woman who could ever hold his heart.

Until she left, she wasn't safe—as Wolf's bullet had so plainly indicated.

"Tell Sawyer I want her to leave. Take the babies and go."

"Why? Because you got shot?"

He thought about the dream of riding in the canyons with his children and the Diablos, and Sawyer watching from afar. "We're not meant to be together," he said, knowing he was speaking a certain truth he'd only just realized in his soul. But the facts had been staring at him for a long time; he just hadn't wanted to acknowledge them. "Tell her what you have to, but convince her she has to leave."

"I'm not telling her that," Ash said hotly. "You tell her. Because I think you're crazy. What about my niece and nephew? You're just going to shuttle them off into hiding?"

What else could he do? "You have a better idea?"

Ash glared at him. "No, I don't!"

He heard a commotion outside his room, laughter, some chatting, a few quick whispered words, and Sawyer walked in, a breath of fresh air in his very dark world. "Hi, Ash." She came over, saw that he was awake, and smiled at him. "You're starting to look like your old self. Yesterday you looked like you'd seen better days."

He studied his beautiful wife. His heart ached when he gazed at her, he wanted so badly to hold her, kiss her. But that would just prolong the agony. "You were here yesterday?"

She nodded.

"I don't remember."

Sawyer sat on the edge of the bed. "They're going to put you in a regular room today. You're out of the woods."

"I'm going," Ash said, with another glare for him. "I don't think you're allowed to have multiple visitors, so I'm going to make myself scarce."

"You're never really scarce," Jace said, "so don't go far. I have a job for you."

"I'm not doing it!" she snapped, and disappeared.

Sawyer pushed his hair back from his forehead. "What are you two up to? You're supposed to be resting."

"Says the pot, who's calling the kettle black." He felt himself relaxing, giving in to her ministrations. He'd missed her so much. "Why aren't you in bed?"

"I just came by to see if you wanted to come with me," she teased, kissing him on the lips.

Of course he wanted to go home with her. He wanted

that more than anything. "No," Jace said, "I'm not going home with you."

"Keep getting strong, cowboy, and I'll bring you home maybe this week. And then the babies. We'll be a family at last."

He grimaced.

"Are you in pain?" Sawyer asked, immediately concerned.

"No." He was in all kinds of pain, and it wasn't from the bullet they'd had to remove from his lung. His heart felt as if it was on fire. "You need to go."

"I know. But I had to see you." She ran a gentle hand along his face. "I can't wait for you to see the babies. They're amazing. And the nurses have been wonderful."

"Sawyer, you have to go into hiding. With the children."

"I know. Running Bear told me. My heart breaks, Jace. I wanted the babies to grow up with your family, the way you had in the tribe. I wanted them to get to know Fiona and Burke and their aunt and all their wonderful uncles and cousins. But I understand."

She didn't entirely understand what was coming, and he felt his heart turn to stone. "We always knew it wasn't destined to work out."

"What wasn't destined to work out?"

"Us." He shrugged. "It's probably a Cash-Callahan curse kind of thing."

"You can put whatever you're thinking out of your head, Jace Callahan. You married me, and we have two wonderful babies. You're going to be a family with us. So if that's the meds talking, then just close your mouth for now, because I'm not listening."

He wanted to smile at her fire, but the situation was far too serious. "Running Bear's words are wise."

"I agree, but he never said we couldn't be a family."

"This is the right thing to do."

"Separating our family will never be the right thing."

Jace thought Sawyer was beginning to sound doubtful, as if she was starting to think he didn't want to be with her. Somehow he had to make her believe that, to get her and the children out of danger. Sawyer wasn't afraid of anything, and that bravery kept her from recognizing the true danger she and the children were in.

"In fact, Fiona thinks we should remarry, renew our vows at Rancho Diablo." Sawyer bent down to kiss him again. He tried not to lean forward, tried not to lengthen the kiss—but it was oh, so hard, like ripping his heart out not to reach for her. "She wants the magic wedding dress to get an airing for the final Callahan bachelor."

He shook his head. "That's not going to happen."

Sawyer pulled away. "You get strong. In the meantime, I'll go take the children to a safe harbor. But I'll be waiting for you, Jace. And I know you'll come. Because if there's anything I know in my heart, it's that I may have won you, but deep inside, you always wanted it that way. No cowboy chases a woman around and makes love to her under the stars for almost two years and then lets her go. So get over whatever it is you've suddenly decided you're afraid of. Because I'm not afraid at all. I know I belong with you, and our children belong with you, too. We're Callahans."

She left with a swirl of Sawyer energy. Jace closed his eyes. Of course she was right; that was one of the things he loved about Sawyer. She was headstrong, spirit-strong and determined. She was brave and fierce, and he was proud of her. There'd never been a woman more suited for him. Sawyer felt like the other half of his whole world, the better half.

But he had to let her go.

Chapter Sixteen

"This is all my fault," Storm said as he drove her and the children to Hell's Colony, Texas. They planned to stay with the other Callahans for a few nights before she was taken on to a safe house. It was June, and the babies were thriving. Sawyer and the babies had been staying in the duplex, and it had been a fun rodeo of learning to breast-feed and juggle baby needs, as well as heal herself.

She wouldn't have traded it for the world.

What she did wish was different was her husband. He came to help at night, but there was a distance between them now. Jace had gone back to work on the ranch before she'd wanted him to, and though he never spoke about his wound, she was pretty sure it still took a toll on him. He didn't talk much, and slept a lot when he wasn't helping her with the babies.

Jason and Ashley kept them very busy. They could be the happiest babies, but when they fussed, it was like a tornado had ripped through the duplex. Jason fussed if Ashley fussed, and vice versa. Neither of them liked to hear the other cry. The situation was made worse by the fact that Jason had colic. When it flared up at night, his cries kept both parents busy and exhausted. The house was small and close, especially with an unhappy baby, and Ashley got upset when she heard her brother wailing.

Lu said it broke her heart to listen to the babies at night. She and Storm could hear them, from the other side of the duplex. They would have needed walls a lot thicker to keep the sound from carrying.

Somehow, Jace managed to calm the babies eventually, and then the three of them slept, both infants on his chest, wrapped together like pieces of pie dough. Sawyer snapped a photo of the babies with him like that, and she treasured it.

When they did talk, it was a bit painful. Jace was pretty focused on her going to Texas, and then into hiding. He constantly made plans about it. Gradually, she'd quit fighting him, ever cognizant of Running Bear's and Fiona's words. Sawyer told herself it didn't matter anymore—ever since the night he'd gotten shot, Jace had been different around her.

Quiet.

"I should never have involved you in my worries about Wolf and the Callahans," her uncle said, breaking into her thoughts. "I was just so certain Wolf was telling me the truth. I couldn't imagine him making so much stuff up. And of course, everyone knows about the bad blood between them."

"I shouldn't have worn the wire. I think that was the part that really bothered Jace. He never said it, but the fact that I'd been recording conversations was hard on him."

"You thought you were acting for the law enforcement agencies that were working the case."

"It doesn't matter, anyway. I should have asked him. I just didn't know him well enough then." Yet she'd known him well enough to let him make love to her every time he'd caught up to her—which was often. In the canyons, when she was supposed to be working. On a mesa... Anywhere she was, somehow he seemed to be, too. Eventually, he would appear, and she'd never told him no. She'd wanted him as much as he'd wanted her.

And now he wanted her gone.

"If he hadn't gotten shot, he wouldn't be so spooked," Storm said. "I can understand his position."

"I can, too, and that makes it even harder. He worries about the babies."

"Sure he does. He worries about you, too."

Sawyer sighed. "Jace is an excellent worrier."

"Well, they've been fighting this battle for a long time. I'm confident that no other family could have withstood Wolf and the cartel as long as the Callahans have."

"What will happen, in the end?"

"I think," Storm said heavily, "that the Callahans are outgunned and outmanned. Once the land across the canyons got overrun with smugglers and the like, I knew I'd made a bad mistake buying it from that old man. No wonder he'd been so eager to sell me his spread. I wondered why he was willing to let it go at such a rock-bottom price, but none of the preliminary information I had on that ranch showed any trouble. Who would have ever imagined that there were miles of tunnels under that place?"

"And we were sitting ducks for Wolf's plan," Sawyer said. "He got you to buy the property, and then had you send me to work at Rancho Diablo for information, while the cartel was busy tunneling underneath. The Callahans still don't know how far they've managed to get, or if the tunnels reach under the canyons to Rancho Diablo yet.

The Feds say it's like a maze under there. A virtual city of catacombs."

"It creeps me out," Storm said. "I'm very happy staying in the duplex these days. But wherever you end up, Lu and I will probably follow. At least for a while. Lu says she wants to help you with the babies."

"It would mean you'd be in hiding," Sawyer said. "Uncle Storm, I can't let you give up your life and hers that way. But I love you for offering."

"Nah," Storm said. "As Lu says, we have nothing better to do. We'd rather be with family than not. But do you have any idea where you're going?"

"No. I'll find out once I'm in Hell's Colony." She was worried, fearful of being away from family. Away from Jace. He wasn't coming with her, that much was clear. He'd always said he didn't want to live the way his parents had, but she'd never thought he'd desert her and the babies.

Then again, they hadn't had much of a marriage.

She wished she could change that.

"The thing is," Storm said, "Wolf used me."

"We know he did," Sawyer replied. "He used all of us to get to the Callahans. And though I never thought I'd fall for it, I did."

"No, I think his plans ran much deeper. You remember how I told you that a long time ago I'd done some horse trading with Fiona?"

Sawyer nodded, and leaned into the backseat to check on Jason and Ashley. "I remember."

"Well, a couple of weeks before Jace got shot, Wolf came to me and mentioned he had some horses he wanted to sell. Wanted to know where the best place for horse trading was."

Sawyer frowned. "What did you tell him?"

"That I didn't know. It didn't work that way, in my experience. If a man had horses to sell, he talked to other people in the business who might know folks who were looking. But as far as I knew, there was no horse outpost or trading center where mass sales occurred around here. Maybe I'm wrong, but it just isn't the way I'd done things." A gentle rain began to fall as they crossed the Texas state line, and Storm turned on the windshield wipers. "Later, I wondered what horses Wolf was talking about. Was the cartel planning to bring horses up from Mexico to sell here?" He shrugged. "I just didn't know. I never asked, either. By then I knew the less time I spent with Wolf Chacon, the happier I was going to be."

"Horses," Sawyer murmured. "It's so weird. Everyone knows you used to breed and train horses. But Wolf could ask anyone in town where to buy or sell them."

"And where would he be keeping horses, if he was planning to buy or sell them? He has no barn, no training area. As far as I know, he and his men seem to float, live off the land."

Sawyer frowned. "I'll ask Jace if he knows. He'll probably call tonight. Maybe he'll be able to figure out exactly what Wolf was after."

"It just doesn't make sense." Storm glanced her way. "I know he loves you, Sawyer. You two are just going through a rough patch right now."

Rough didn't begin to describe it. Yet she'd always known there was a heavy price to being a Callahan. "Thank you for taking us to Texas, Uncle Storm."

The sky turned darker as night fell. Soon it was almost pitch-black. "I'm going to need to feed the babies soon."

"I know." He pulled off the highway and headed down a deserted road.

"Where are we going?" Sawyer asked.

"Just keeping away from prying eyes."

"You think we were followed?" Fear jumped into her heart. She couldn't bear it if anything happened to the babies. "Surely we weren't!"

"I don't think so. But it pays to be careful."

He stopped the truck, switching it off.

"You don't have to stop driving." Sawyer looked at her uncle. "I can get in the backseat and feed the babies."

He let out a deep sigh. "Sawyer, I'm not taking you to Texas."

"Why? What are you talking about?"

A truck pulled up behind them.

"This is just the way it has to be. I'm sorry I couldn't tell you, but I was asked not to." He got out of the vehicle.

"Uncle Storm!"

He opened the back door, unstrapped one of the baby carriers and lifted it out.

"What are you doing?" Sawyer jumped from the truck to run around and face her uncle.

"Shh," a voice said next to her, and she whirled.

"Jace!"

"Thanks, Storm," Jace said. "Put the babies in the back. Sawyer, do you have everything? Anything else I need to get out of the truck?"

"I have everything." She looked at him, shocked to find him there. "What's going on?"

"Get in the truck. Quickly." He shook Storm's hand. "*Vaya con Dios,* Storm. I can't thank you enough."

"No problem. Take care of my little girl." He kissed the top of Sawyer's head, pushed her toward Jace. "Mind your uncle, girl, and get in the truck. I'll see you again one day."

Sawyer hopped into the dark truck, which was exactly like the one Storm was driving. The whole transfer had taken less than sixty seconds—and the next thing she knew, Jace was behind the wheel. He gave her a long, sexy smooch and then a rascally smile, obviously pleased with himself.

"You didn't really think I was letting you go without me, did you?"

He turned the truck down the dirt road. Sawyer glanced back at her uncle, who was driving the opposite way. It looked as if someone was sitting next to him, though she could barely see in the dark. "Yes, I thought you were sending me and the babies off. I didn't know when or if I'd ever see you again." She glared at him. "Why all the secrecy? Couldn't you have given me a little hint? I've cried because of you, you ape!"

"I'm sorry about that. But we had to keep everything very quiet. Storm agreed to help me, and I couldn't endanger him. Even Lu didn't know."

Sawyer took a deep breath. "Never mind. I don't care what rabbits you pulled out of hats to make this happen."

"I have no intention of living without my family."

"You're taking us to Texas?"

"Actually, we're not going to Texas. Storm is going to Hell's Colony. He's the decoy."

"And conveniently, has a body decoy in the front seat." It was all coming together—even the quick switch on the dirt road, the duplicate trucks.

"He'll continue on to Hell's Colony, and then my cousin's going to fly him back in the family jet. By the time

Wolf's men figure out we've pulled a switch, you and I and the babies will be long gone."

"Never to be seen again?" Sudden fear made Sawyer's pulse leap. It sounded so scary. "Actual hiding, like your parents? And the Callahans?"

"For now," he said grimly. "We shot Wolf. We're on his short, fast list of enemies."

"*I* shot Wolf. *You* had nothing to do with it." She thought about the past and everything she knew about the Callahans. "I'm not the only sister-in-law who shot your uncle, either. So why has he pursued us so diligently?"

"When Rhein was arrested, he spent some time being interrogated by Sheriff Cartwright. The sheriff learned that Wolf took it particularly hard about the pink Taser. He felt like we weren't taking him seriously. That a little pink toy gun wasn't a respectful way to shoot a man."

"So he would have been happier if I'd used a Sig Sauer 9 mm?"

"Apparently so."

"The egos in your family tree never cease to amaze me," Sawyer murmured. "If it helps, I'm sorry. I shouldn't have shot him, I guess, but he came into my house uninvited, and I'm never going to be the kind of girl who sits helplessly and waits to be rescued."

Jace laughed. "Fine by me. Personally, I admired your approach."

"Except that now you're going into hiding because of me."

"With you, babe. And my children. No worries."

She nodded and looked out the window. There were worries, plenty of them—but Jace was with her now, and their babies had their family.

It was worth shooting ugly old Wolf.

THEY ENDED UP in a small house in Oklahoma, in a small town so far from anything, Sawyer imagined she could walk for days and not see another soul. If Wolf or his band of weirdos ever tried to find them, they'd have to go out of their way to do it. They were so far out in the country, it was a thirty minute drive for groceries. She'd have to go into "town" to get any mail—not that they got any at the post office, of course. They never would.

Jace was quiet all the time, and she could tell he was thinking about his family, and how he was walking in their footsteps, hiding out from an enemy who never seemed to rest.

There wasn't any way to change it now.

Anyway, she knew Jace hadn't been entirely forth-right about why Wolf was in such a killing rage. He'd thought she'd been on his side, that she and Uncle Storm had cheated him. He felt betrayed, and was determined a price would be paid for that betrayal.

Jace rolled over in the bed next to her, reaching to hold her close to him. The babies slept on pallets in the same room. She wasn't certain what they were going to do when Jason and Ashley got a couple months older. There were no cribs, and no reason to buy any furniture; they weren't sure how long they'd be here. Or anywhere.

For now, the road was their home. They'd be here until a signal was sent, and then they'd move on to the next safe house.

"It's okay," Jace said. "I can feel you thinking about it, but let it go, Sawyer. Nothing matters but the fact that we're safe, we're together."

She snuggled up against him, grateful that he was there, that she wasn't walking this road alone. "I'm glad you're with me."

"That's right," he murmured, nearly asleep. "Tell me I'm your Prince Charming."

"You could say that," she said, kissing him. "It's most likely true."

"I know. But it's more fun when you admit it," he murmured. "Now go to sleep, angel mama."

"If I was an angel, you wouldn't have gotten shot because of me."

"Trust me, you're an angel. It's not your fault my uncle shot me. Wolf's been trying to pick one of us off for a long time. I don't know that him shooting me was payback for the little zap you gave him." Jace kissed her hand. "I do know you're the only woman for me. Now go to sleep."

"Jace?"

"Hmm?"

"When you showed up with your truck, it really did feel like you were my Prince Charming. Fairy-tale ride-off-into-the-sunset and all that. I was so happy to see you."

"Good princes have plans. And I planned on being your Prince Charming."

She giggled, and he held her close, and for the moment, Sawyer felt like the luckiest girl in the world.

IN THE NIGHT, when the babies awakened for their feeding, Jace helped Sawyer diaper them, then rock them back to sleep. These were the moments she'd been missing, had been so afraid might never happen. She loved seeing her big strong husband hold Ashley and Jason.

"You're beautiful," he told her. "There's nothing more beautiful to a man than watching a woman take care of his children."

She smiled. "I was just thinking pretty much the same thing about you. I was so worried we'd never be together."

"Nothing to worry about anymore."

His mobile phone rang, and they looked at each other. "An odd hour for someone to get in touch," Sawyer said. A call at 2:00 a.m. seemed like a bad omen, but she didn't voice her worry aloud.

Jace grabbed his phone off the nightstand. "Ash? What's going on?"

Sawyer put the babies gently back onto their pallets to sleep, and laid blankets over them. She rubbed their backs as Jace went outside to talk.

He came back in, began putting on his boots.

"What's happening?" Sawyer asked fearfully.

"We're going back home."

"To Rancho Diablo? What's happened?"

Jace walked around the room a couple times, stared down at his babies. Looked at Sawyer, seeming undecided. She held her breath, waited.

"Fiona's had a heart attack." His aunt needed him, needed all of them. "All I know is that right now, we belong at Rancho Diablo."

Family meant strength, and no one had given them more strength than Fiona.

Chapter Seventeen

"I don't want anybody fussing over me," Fiona announced loudly to anyone within earshot, particularly medical personnel, and Jace thought his aunt had never been more stubborn.

"And I especially want to know why you're back here, when you're supposed to be *in hiding*," she said, the last two words directed at him softly, urgently. "What do you not understand about your present circumstances? It wasn't that long ago that you were in this hospital, in worse shape than me."

He sat down next to his aunt, took her hand in his. "Sawyer said family's all that matters. She said I should be here with you."

"Doesn't mean you had to bring her and the children back, too. We went through a lot of planning to get that mission just right." She sniffed. "You don't want to give me any peace in my old age? First you get shot and now you're here."

He knew he shouldn't have brought Sawyer and the babies right back into the jaws of danger. He remembered the knife in the wedding cake, and every other warning Wolf and his men had sent his way. But he couldn't leave Sawyer alone with the babies in an unfamiliar place—

and Sawyer had told him if he tried to leave her, she'd follow him back in a taxi and run up such a bill on him he'd be paying for it until the next Christmas ball. Sawyer had also reminded him in no uncertain terms that she'd emptied her bank account to win him, and now that she had him, she wasn't sending him into Wolf's clutches without backup.

Which she considered herself to be.

Jace smiled at Fiona's grumbling and rubbed her hand. "So how's the ticker?"

"Better now that you're here," she said begrudgingly. "Family makes me strong. You are my greatest weakness."

"It's not a weakness," he said fondly. "We'll get you back on your feet, and then you can shoo us off again."

"I don't think it'll work," Fiona said. "Your parents stayed away. I also got my sister, Molly, and Jeremiah safely off. But my luck broke down with you, and I sense you're probably here to stay under my feet for good."

"Could be worse."

"Could be," Fiona said, closing her eyes. "Frankly, I think you took my heart with you and that's why it broke. That's probably the meds talking, though."

"The doctors say you didn't actually have a heart attack, more like a cardiac event that could have been triggered by some of your other meds. Nothing that will keep you off the ranch more than a couple of days. You're strong as an ox, Fiona."

"Stronger," she said, her voice suddenly light and tired, and Jace sat rubbing her fingers until she fell asleep.

Fiona had a point, though. Sawyer and the babies shouldn't be here. The thing was, he was pretty certain if he sent his wife and babies away, he'd end up like Fiona, with a badly broken heart.

JACE WALKED INTO the kitchen at Rancho Diablo, astonished to see his sister holding little Ashley and Galen holding Jason. "What are they doing here?" He took his daughter from Ash, who protested, then kissed her namesake on the cheek. "I thought I left my family at the duplex."

"Through the wonders of automation," Galen said, "they ended up here when their mother drove them to the ranch."

"And where is my beautiful wife?" Jace asked.

"Cleaning out the far foreman's bungalow," Ash said. "Don't worry, I sent help with her. But a woman has to put her house together the way she wants it to be, or it never feels like home, you know."

This wasn't good. Jace stared at his sister. "You don't mean the foreman's bungalow near the canyons?"

Ash nodded. "That was the one Sawyer chose. She said she liked the way the sun rose over the canyons there."

It was also closest to Wolf and the tunnels and everything bad Jace didn't want around her and his family. He handed Ashley back to her aunt. "Could you watch them for another thirty minutes? I need to speak to Sawyer."

"Sure. No problem." Ash greedily took her niece back in her arms, and Jace went out the door, jumping in his truck and speeding off to the bungalow like a madman.

He burst into the house, startling Mavis, Corinne and Nadine.

"Mercy!" Corinne exclaimed. "Do that again and we'll all end up in the hospital with Fiona!"

"Very sorry, ladies." He gave them his most apologetic smile and looked around for his wife. "Where's Sawyer?"

"She went back to the main house," Mavis said. "Didn't you pass her?"

He looked around the bungalow, amazed by how fresh and homey everything looked. "You ladies have made this place look better than it ever has."

"Oh, we just helped Sawyer put up curtains and the like," Nadine said. "She called into town for what she wanted, while you were with Fiona."

"Go see the nursery," Corinne said, her tone gleeful. "Sawyer said she'd had a long time to think about how she wanted the nursery to look, and we think it's perfect!"

He went down the hall, his heart sinking. Sawyer didn't understand—they weren't staying here. Once Fiona turned the corner, they'd go back on the road. He shouldn't have brought his wife and the children home, but he'd wanted them with him, couldn't have borne to leave them alone in a strange place where they didn't know anyone, didn't know the town.

Although he knew Sawyer well enough to believe she would have done just fine.

He walked into the nursery, his pulse hitching briefly as he saw Sawyer's dreams for their children expressed in the amazing decor. It looked like a real home, a place where children would be happy and secure in their world.

They would have nothing like this in hiding, and his heart broke a little. For the first time, he understood why his parents had chosen to leave them with Running Bear, among the tribe.

Because they'd wanted this—stability and comfort and continuity—for their children. Tears welled in his eyes as he recognized the full weight of their heartbreak.

He felt as if he stood at an intersection, with each road heading a different way, and he had to choose the right path for his family. Jace looked at the pink and blue painted signs, one reading Ashley and one Jason. He took in the plaid valances that hung over the white cribs, which had pink sheets for Ashley, blue for Jason, with knitted baby blankets to match. A portrait of black mustangs hung on the back wall, along with pictures of the babies and one of him and Sawyer. A photo of all the Chacon Callahans stood on the dresser. Each crib had a mobile with dainty stuffed animals hanging above it: puppies, kittens, giraffes and bunnies that danced when he touched them.

It was a room for babies to start out in, get their footing in life. And suddenly, he realized Sawyer had no plans on going anywhere.

She'd finally found her home.

SAWYER WENT INTO the attic at Rancho Diablo, sent by Fiona, because, as Jace's "redoubtable aunt" said, her curiosity was killing her. So Sawyer went, slowly going up the fabled staircase to find the treasured wedding gown she never thought she'd wear.

But Fiona said she'd feel better—enormously better—if Sawyer tried it on. Sawyer had assured her that she was happily married, and there was no need for her to do so. At which point Fiona had said that only one Callahan bride hadn't tried on the wedding gown, and that was a special occasion upon which no magic was needed.

"But you," she'd told Sawyer over the phone, "could use a giant dose of magical assistance."

So here I am, Sawyer thought. *In the attic where all*

the magic gets stored for loading up the magic wand when necessary.

It must be necessary if Fiona's sent me here.

She turned on the light and went to the closet, opening the door slowly. Just as Fiona had instructed, a billowy white bag hung there, the contents of which could only be the Callahan dress of dreams. Sawyer undid the zipper apprehensively, reminding herself that she was married with children, and no magic was needed.

Except that Fiona seemed to think Sawyer could use a sparkly dose of fairy dust. She opened the bag and drew out a lovely gown that seemed to shimmer as she held it against her. In the reflection from the cheval mirror, the dress glowed, inviting her to try it on.

What could it hurt? She'd be making Jace's aunt happy when she most needed to be. "Oh, for heaven's sake," Sawyer mumbled. "It's just a dress, no different than if Fiona had asked me to run down to the store and try on a pair of jeans. She's not asking that much."

So she pulled off her clothes and stepped into the dress, drawing the twinkling bodice up, sliding her arms through the lovely lace sleeves.

The gown seemed to zip itself up, encasing her in a magical whisper of fairy-tale romance.

She'd never felt so beautiful, so at peace within herself. So Callahan.

Somehow she felt all the misgivings and worries slide away, never to return.

Jace walked in, put his hands on her waist. "You look beautiful, babe, but you always are to me."

She smiled. She'd expected the vision; all the Callahan brides talked about them. Those were just tales they told each other, surely. Still, she felt Jace's warmth and the strength of his hands holding her, and was amazed by how real the vision seemed.

"As beautiful as you are right now," he said, kissing her shoulder, "I never thought you were more beautiful than when you had our children."

"Jace," she murmured, touched.

"It's true. I'd always heard motherhood made a woman glow with inner beauty, but I fell in love with you even more the day I saw you pregnant. Which was the first day you came back." He turned her and kissed her gently. Sawyer was shocked by how a vision could smell as delicious as her husband did in her arms, feel the way her husband felt when he held her. If this was a dream, she needed to wake up soon, or she was going to end up like the other Callahan brides, chattering and giggling over her own special "vision."

"The best part is we're together forever," Jace said. "I knew that when I saw the nursery at the bungalow. You're not hitting the road. You're not going into hiding."

"No," Sawyer murmured. "I belong here, just as much as you do."

He smiled, sexy and handsome. "I've waited a long time to hear you say that, babe."

"It's true. Wherever you are, that's my home. I love you, Jace."

Happiness lit his eyes, and Sawyer expected him to disappear, to evanesce with the fading light that was streaming in the windows. But he stayed strong in her arms, holding her, his touch warm and strong. And magical.

Because it was magic. And no matter how hard the road had been, no matter how hard it would be in the future, they were together.

Forever.

"Can I help you out of this gown before it disappears?" Jace asked, kissing her again. "I've heard a rumor that it vanishes when the fancy takes it."

Sawyer smiled. "I think that's just a fairy tale, a Fiona legend."

And maybe it was a legend. It didn't matter. All that mattered was that she had her Callahan.

And wasn't that the stuff of dreams?

"Disappear, husband, so I can change," she said, and Jace grinned.

"I'd offer to help, but I know you'd like to be alone to enjoy the bibbidi-bobbidi-boo awhile longer." He kissed her again and headed down the attic stairs, and Sawyer turned back to the mirror, hardly able to believe the enchanting loveliness of the fabulous wedding dress.

To her surprise, the gown suddenly tightened, warmed a bit, then felt as if it was falling away. Sawyer stared at her image in the cheval mirror, absolutely stunned when the gown evanesced and reshaped itself into an entirely new garment.

She was wearing black leggings and a bulletproof vest, with a black, long-sleeved T-shirt overtop.

And that's when she knew the fairy-tale happy ending wasn't yet hers.

Chapter Eighteen

Reality brought Jace crashing to earth the next day when he paid a visit to Wolf. Jace didn't tell Sawyer when he left. He knew she would either send a team along or insist on coming with him herself. Probably would have ripped up the magic wedding dress and burned it in a blazing bonfire in the canyons if he'd tried to leave her behind.

After seeing his wife wearing the splendid dress, he fully intended to allow her the magical moment of which all Callahan brides dreamed. He wouldn't take that from her.

But first things first, and he had a bullet and a scarred lung to thank Wolf for—not to mention a warning to deliver, since Sawyer was absolutely determined to stay at Rancho Diablo with him and the babies. She said he was a family man, and that was what she loved most about him, and that he wouldn't be happy living out of duffel bags and backpacks. That he was more the soccer coach and ballet recital kind of dad.

He loved her all the more for knowing him as well as she did.

"Wolf Chacon!" he yelled when he got to the stone and fire ring. Many moons ago Running Bear had brought all the siblings here to meet their Callahan cousins. He'd told them this was their home now, that they would hold Rancho Diablo in their hearts. Their parents' mission had become theirs.

This was the perfect place to face his uncle. Jace figured that as soon as he'd left the ranch and ridden toward the canyons, his progress had been marked.

When his uncle appeared at the fire ring, Jace knew he'd been right.

"You want to see me?" Wolf demanded.

"Damn right I do."

"Come for another bullet, nephew?"

Jace smiled grimly. "Where are your bodyguards? The minions who put knives in wedding cakes and do all your dirty work?"

Wolf laughed. "Don't worry. They're never far away."

Jace thought about the secret passage in Rancho Diablo's kitchen he'd never known about, the missing Diablos and the silver treasure, which was supposedly hidden on the ranch. He thought about the kindness and gentleness of the people of the town of Diablo, who were always willing to help, and he thought about his family, every last one of them committed to the heartbeat of Rancho Diablo.

"You really don't understand, do you?" Jace said. "You can't ever win, Wolf. You can't possess Rancho Diablo. It's a *spirit,* a spirit wind that can't be held by anyone."

"You've been listening to Running Bear's nonsense far too long. Trust me, land is easily held. I won't have any problem doing it."

"You will," Jace said. "You will because you don't understand the land. To you it's a thing that can be bought and sold, drained of its resources and life."

"It's called making money, son. If you hadn't fallen

for Running Bear's fairy tales, you'd be making money instead of working for your cousins for nothing."

Jace frowned. "You can't understand the calling of the spirit."

"Blah, blah, blah." Wolf laughed, pulled his black cowboy hat down over his eyes. "I understand the calling of money. Cash is king. If you were a smarter man, you'd learn that lesson. And that wife of yours—"

"Tread carefully," Jace warned.

"That wife of yours is just like her uncle, always trying to do the right thing. Gets folks in trouble every time. You see, when you believe that people are inherently good, you fail to understand their dark side. Everyone has a dark side, Jace. Sawyer hasn't seen yours. But it's there. Eventually, it will trip you up."

Jace's skin chilled despite the hot sun. "And then what? You think we'll join your cause?"

Wolf shrugged. "Either that or I'll just keep picking you off, one by one. Or two by two, in your case, right? You have two little babies by that sweet bodyguard wife—"

Jace's fist slammed into Wolf's jaw so fast he didn't see it coming. Wolf lay crumpled by the fire, stunned for a moment, before he got to his feet.

"You shouldn't have done that."

Jace shrugged. "Whatever trouble you have with me, you stay away from my wife."

"Everyone has a dark side, and she's shown hers," Wolf said, rubbing his jaw. "She's fair game now."

It was too easy. Jace could kill his uncle right here, and no one could stop him. Wolf didn't think he'd do it; that's why he'd come alone. He knew quite well that

Running Bear had said none of the Callahans were to harm their uncle.

But Wolf was right: Jace did have a dark side.

And killing Wolf would be so sweet.

"WHERE HAVE YOU been?" Sawyer asked anxiously when he walked inside the bunkhouse.

"Out checking on a few things. Everything good?" He glanced at the babies, snug in the laps of Ash and of Fiona. Recently released from the hospital, Fiona moved more slowly now, and complained that they were making her sit around too much for no reason at all. Ash stayed very close to her, so close that only Burke ever really got any time with his wife without Ash hanging around.

"Everything's fine." Sawyer put on a hat and her boots while he watched her suspiciously. He looked at the tight black leggings and long-sleeved T-shirt she wore—pretty warm stuff for weather that was as hot as a pistol outside. Not to mention that she looked as if she was on her way to a raid.

"Are we supposed to be going somewhere?" Jace asked.

"You're going shopping for the grand wedding I'm throwing," Fiona said, beaming. "You realize I got up off my deathbed for your marriage, which will be the event of the year."

Sawyer glanced at him. "She's very excited about us saying our vows again."

Now that sounded better. For a moment, his wife's serious face had puzzled him; he thought he'd forgotten something important. "Shopping it is." He looked at Sawyer's clothes a bit doubtfully, thinking his wife really looked more like she was in recon mode than shopping mode. "I really don't like you to be out long. You should still be resting." He kissed both his babies on their small downy heads.

"Yes, but you don't like me to be out without you, either, so I have to wait for you to bring your muscles home. And you were gone longer than I expected," Sawyer said, glancing out the window, though he wasn't sure what she was looking for. "So now we have to hurry. The sun will go down in about an hour."

What the sun's positioning had to do with wedding preparations, he couldn't have said, but he kissed his babies again, kissed his aunt, tugged his sister's platinum ponytail and took his wife's hand to lead her out the door. "We'll be back in a bit," he told his family. "Wedding stuff should be a piece of cake."

Ash laughed. "Keep thinking that, brother."

Sawyer hurried to the truck. She hopped in and buckled her seat belt. "We're making a detour to the house you bought from my uncle."

That wasn't so strange, he supposed. Though the Callahan conglomerate now owned Storm's ranch, maybe she wanted to return for sentimental reasons. He backed up the truck. "I thought we were going to do fantasy bride stuff?"

She shook her head. "You can call this fantasy bride stuff if you want to. Just hurry. We don't have much time, because if we don't get to the stores to pick out the stuff Fiona wants us to, she'll know we didn't go. But we have a very small errand to run first."

"I guess all wisdom will be revealed to me in due time," Jace said, heading for Storm's old ranch. The place was probably thick with Feds, and cartel thugs, too, since it was practically deserted these days. He wanted no part of his family being over here until the ranch was cleaned up.

Storm had been right to move away.

Sometimes Jace thought Ash was right, and that they should dynamite the land across the canyons, cover it over with concrete and turn it into Callahan Rodeo Land, to flush out the bad guys.

"Speaking of fantasy bride stuff, you sure did look like an angel in Fiona's magic rag."

Sawyer gasped. "You can't call it that! Your aunt would be appalled if she thought you were making fun of the magic. And anyway, you aren't supposed to see me wearing the gown before the big day. I'm pretending you didn't, and that you were just my special Callahan vision."

He laughed. "It was very good luck for me. In fact, it was all I could do not to make that fairy-tale frock disappear from your goddesslike body and make princely love to you."

"Every Callahan bride has supposedly seen the man of her dreams when she's worn the gown."

"You did see me. Only it was even better, because I was there in the flesh." He reached for her hand, raised it to his lips, kissed her fingers. "You can't believe everything my aunt tells you. Most of it's wonderfully childlike, romantic tales, to get us to do what she wants us to do."

"What she believes is best for you," Sawyer amended. "Her track record is pretty amazing so far."

"I know. So what's this we're going to see?"

"Remember when Ash commandeered the treasure-hunting equipment from the trespasser?"

"Oh, yeah. I forgot all about that." Jace laughed out

loud. "My sister has nerves of steel. Did the guy come wanting his equipment back?"

"No, surprisingly. And that got my curiosity up. Remember how Uncle Storm got used by Wolf to buy this ranch, so Wolf could get access to the land through him? Obviously, Wolf didn't want to buy it. He doesn't have the resources, and the land he really wants is Rancho Diablo. Which he wanted access to."

"Through your uncle's land, and this land." Jace parked the truck. "I'm with you so far."

"I was thinking about why he wanted my uncle to help him so much, and then got so mad at me when he felt I'd betrayed him. And I thought it was odd that the man from whom Ash took the equipment never made a stink about it. Plus I remembered Uncle Storm telling me that Wolf was always asking him a lot of questions about selling horses, buying horses, etc."

Jace followed his wife as she pulled the metal detector from the back of the truck. "I don't know if it's a good idea for you to have that out here. Wolf's thugs have eyes on everything."

"It's okay. I don't really care." She took off at a good clip across the ranch, carrying the equipment.

She was scaring the hell out of him. A tingle hit him, a sense of karma colliding—and suddenly, he remembered the dream he'd had in the hospital, which had seemed so much like a vision. He and Sawyer had been here—only she'd been atop a mesa, and he'd been far away, riding a Diablo. It was an impossible dream, because the Diablos hadn't been seen or heard in a long time—but a sudden premonition told Jace there was danger here. He followed Sawyer quickly, glad he was armed, wishing he had backup.

Once Sawyer reached a particular destination—he happened to know that it was near the cave Galen had been held in some months ago, but didn't want to say so to Sawyer, because with his luck, she'd decide to go spelunking—she stopped and looked toward Rancho Diablo. "It's beautiful, no matter where you stand to look at it."

He eyed the seven chimneys of the main house, rising in the distance. "It is."

"If you stood here and looked at that long enough, you might wish you lived there."

"I do live there."

She ignored his lame attempt at humor. "One day I'm going to take our babies riding on this land," Sawyer said, "and it's going to be free and safe."

He hoped she was right, yet his scalp prickled all the same. "Let me carry this thing. It's too heavy for you." He took the metal detector from her, still not sure why they needed it, but not about to interrupt his wife when she was on a mission. Everyone had a holy grail, and if this was hers, far be it from him to throw a wrench in the works. He glanced around, made certain they weren't being followed as she strode toward the canyons.

When Sawyer stopped at the edge, looking over, he gulped. "Please don't do what I think you're going to do."

"That's where the Diablos run," she whispered. "This is the yellow brick road."

"Yes, but we haven't seen them in months."

"I know." She looked across the canyons at the burned-out farmhouse, then turned back to stare at Rancho Diablo. "If you had always lived there, and looked across these canyons, you might have wished life had gone differently for you."

"Maybe, but Rancho Diablo's been built up over many years. Three, four decades?"

"And all those years, that farmer watched. And you know who else watched?"

"Wolf," Jace said.

"That's right. The man who lived in that house was a friend of Wolf's. All those years, he was a spy for him, until Wolf was ready to put his plan into action."

"How do you know all this?" Jace's heart began an uncomfortable thumping.

"Because I asked him. I looked at the property deed at the county courthouse and found the gentleman's name, and after I got out of the hospital and had time to think things through, I went and asked him everything I wanted to know. When you were shot, I knew we hadn't heard the whole story, and I knew someone else had to have pieces of it."

Jace swallowed hard. "You were supposed to be resting."

"And you were supposed to stay alive so you could be my husband," Sawyer told him. "I knew it wasn't my uncle who'd given up information. He didn't know anything. So someone had been feeding information to Wolf. The only person who could have kept a closer eye on things than my uncle was the man who owned that land over there. And that's exactly what happened. He was quite willing to tell me everything, because Wolf reneged on his promise of land and Rancho Diablo silver."

"Still, why are we standing out here with Ash's nefariously acquired equipment?"

"Because," Sawyer said, "we both know the silver is important, but it's not the ranch's most prized possession. Life according to Running Bear states that the most important part of the ranch is the spirit. The *spirits*. And that's what your uncle simply can't get through his thick skull."

"I just love how your mind works," Jace said admiringly. "All this time I thought you were just a gorgeous face, a redhead with a body to drive me mad."

"You thought nothing of the sort."

"I swear I did."

"Good. Hang on for the ride, cowboy. I'm about to drive you really mad."

And with that, she disappeared off the side of the canyon. Jace cursed, looked over the edge, knew that the only woman he could ever love had figured out there was a stairway of rocks leading downward.

Which meant she'd been hanging around over here by herself, with no Callahan protection, because she was determined to clear her uncle's name—and hers.

She still didn't accept that she was a true Callahan.

"We're going to fix that," he muttered, checking his gun. "And somehow I don't think we're going wedding shopping today."

So he followed her.

Chapter Nineteen

It seemed they'd walked for miles in a tunnel Sawyer had found. Jace didn't even want to think about the fact that his wife was basically charting unknown territory in a recently dug maze leading from Storm's ranch to a point unknown.

"I should send you home," Jace said. "You're taking ten years off my life."

"Shh," Sawyer said over her shoulder. She'd pulled a flashlight from a holster he hadn't realized she was wearing, and shone it in front of them. "Walls have ears, they say."

It was definitely true at Rancho Diablo, but he wasn't sure if these dirt-packed walls had any listening devices. "So when you were supposed to be home resting and taking care of our children, you were playing detective?"

"I am a bodyguard," she reminded him. "Just because we had children doesn't mean I stopped trying to protect the family."

"Remember when we had that discussion about you being a stay-at-home mom?"

"And you volunteered to be Mr. Mom? Hold this." She handed him the flashlight, bent down to put her ear against the dirt floor.

"I don't think it's going to work," Jace said. "I can't stay at home with the kids and keep an eye on you, too."

"This is the easy part. Learning to breast-feed was much harder. Rewarding, but harder."

"What are we looking for? I sense you aren't playing underground Miss Marple just for fun. We lugged this treasure-hunting device with us for a reason."

"I'm not sure what I'm looking for. It just seemed like a good thing to have, since someone was on the property using it. For all I know, Wolf's found the fabled Callahan silver treasure." She rose, pushed on a cave wall. Something moved slightly, and he helped her push, and a crude door opened.

And there, fenced off from the canyons they so loved, were the black Diablo mustangs. A lone silver mare was enclosed in a pen, and several stallions had tried to kick their way to her. There were bloody marks along the pen walls and the fencing that blocked them from the canyons. The stallions stayed close to the mare—a trap to keep them from trying to escape. The Diablos were hidden away from the sun and the wind and the independence they loved.

"Oh, no," Sawyer murmured under her breath, and before Jace could stop her, she was in the middle of the herd, little more than her red hair visible among the black horses. He threw down the metal detector and followed her, his gun at the ready.

Suddenly, as if someone had shouted "Freedom!" the Diablos surged past him. They bolted for the wide-open spaces beyond the mouth of the tunnel as Sawyer held open a heavy wooden gate. A few stallions stayed tight to the pen of the silver mare, but after a moment, even they gave in to the desire for liberty. Soon the underground corral was empty.

"Come on!" Jace muttered to Sawyer. "As soon as those mustangs hit the canyons, Wolf's going to know we freed his stolen treasure."

"Just a minute." She approached the silver mare, which was looking patiently over the pen wall at her. "Come on, girl."

"Sawyer," Jace said, "we don't have time. We're on stolen time, in fact."

"Don't leave the metal detector behind. Ash will want her equipment back." Sawyer swung up on the silver mare and he opened the pen. "See you at home, husband."

"You're not going without me. I'm riding shotgun this time," he said, grabbing the metal detector and whistling at the cave entrance. A lone mustang stallion danced nearby, nervous, ready to run, and Jace swung up on its back. "Head for home and don't look back for any reason at all."

They shot out of the underground maze and tore across the land toward Rancho Diablo. Jace glanced behind them to see if they were being followed. *Not yet, not yet.*

He heard hooves behind him. "Go!" he yelled at Sawyer, glancing over his shoulder again. Running Bear rode a hundred lengths back, before wheeling his horse to protect their departure. Jace rode hard to cover Sawyer, praying that she'd make it at least to the perimeter of Rancho Diablo. A moment later, the sight of his five brothers and Ash galloping toward them nearly stopped his heart.

It was going to be all right.

In fact, it was going to be even better than all right.

He and Sawyer were finally home.

"Just so you know, you nearly gave me heart failure," Ash said to Jace as she stood beside him two days later at the altar. He'd chosen Ash to be his best man because she simply was—and Sawyer had agreed, saying Ash could also be her maid of honor. If anyone could handle both honorary duties, it was her sister-in-law.

Ash had spied the Diablos running in the canyons, and from her perch on the bunkhouse roof, she could see that the horses were wild with some kind of pent-up panic. She'd told her brothers that something was wrong, that the mysticism felt weak and somehow almost invisible, and they'd instantly ridden for the canyons.

Jace had never been so glad to see his family in his life. At that moment, as he'd spotted them riding to the rescue, he'd known Sawyer would make it home. With Running Bear at their back, they stood a chance.

Somehow, incredibly, Wolf's men never even put up a fight. Which was a warning in and of itself: Wolf had never suspected that they would find the underground corral that shut the Diablos away from the canyons they called home. He'd planned to sell them over the border, no doubt, which was why he'd asked Storm the questions about horse trading, and why he'd wanted Storm's ranch available to him to hide the Diablos—except that Storm had sold the ranch to the Callahans, thus dashing Wolf's hopes to make a huge fortune.

"You only think you nearly had heart failure, Ash. It was my wife who…never mind. I can't think about it." He swallowed hard, still shocked by what Sawyer had done. She was a Callahan bride for sure.

"You definitely married the right woman." Ash giggled. "I believe of all my brothers, you won the prize. Kind of funny, isn't it, since she had to buy you at Fiona's Christmas auction just to get a date with you?"

He smiled. "I'm a fortunate man."

And it was a perfect day to marry a woman who had

completely stolen his heart. Fiona and Company had decorated the ranch splendidly, with satin bows, and torches ready to be lit at nightfall, when the party would begin. White lights twinkled like stars along the corrals, where more bows topped every post. He didn't think the ranch had ever looked more magical.

But then Sawyer came down the aisle on her uncle's arm, with Storm beaming from ear to ear, and Jace's own grin felt as if it stretched a mile wild. His bride wore the magic wedding dress, which looked totally different than it had the other day. The gown was white and simple, elegant with lace sleeves and a long train, and two Callahan nieces tossed pink petals before Sawyer as she walked toward him.

He was the luckiest man in the world.

"You're beautiful," he told Sawyer when she came to stand beside him. "The magic wedding dress is perfect on you." He didn't know about Fiona's tale of magic, but his wife was so lovely, so breathtakingly sexy, that he couldn't wait to hold her in his arms as soon as possible.

She smiled. "It's more magical than you'll ever know. I have a little story to tell you one day about this dress, and how it led us to the Diablos."

"We'll have many years for you to tell me this fairy tale, and I look forward to hearing every word."

"It's my own chapter for the Callahan books. By the way, I definitely got the sexiest bridegroom on the planet. I might even say I won my sexy groom."

"You've definitely won my heart." He couldn't wait for the vows to be said, so he kissed her, feeling that special magic zip between them. "This is the happiest day of my life, besides the day our children were born," he told her softly. "I love you so much, Sawyer."

"I love you, too," Sawyer replied, and Jace knew he was the happiest man in New Mexico.

They said the vows, and Sawyer's eyes sparkled as he slipped the wedding ring on her finger. She did the same for him, and Jace thought hearing the deacon pronounce them man and wife was the moment he'd waited for all his life. Colorful paper hearts floated on the air as their friends and family celebrated. The babies were handed to them so he could hold Ashley, while Sawyer held Jason. And that's the way their wedding photos looked: one big happy family in a wonderful place called Rancho Diablo.

The sound of hooves thundering through the canyons filtered to them on the summer breeze. Jace smiled at Sawyer, the woman who'd made everything possible for him. He was finally the family man he'd always wanted to be.

And it was more magical than he could have ever imagined. It was enchanting, a miracle.

Best of all, it was family. His family.

Forever.

* * * *

There's one more story in the
CALLAHAN COWBOYS *miniseries!*
Will Ash finally get her man in
SWEET CALLAHAN HOMECOMING?
Coming April 2014,
only from Harlequin American Romance!

REQUEST YOUR FREE BOOKS!
2 FREE NOVELS PLUS 2 FREE GIFTS!

HARLEQUIN

American Romance

LOVE, HOME & HAPPINESS

YES! Please send me 2 FREE Harlequin® American Romance® novels and my 2 FREE gifts (gifts are worth about $10). After receiving them, if I don't wish to receive any more books, I can return the shipping statement marked "cancel." If I don't cancel, I will receive 4 brand-new novels every month and be billed just $4.74 per book in the U.S. or $5.24 per book in Canada. That's a savings of at least 14% off the cover price! It's quite a bargain! Shipping and handling is just 50¢ per book in the U.S. and 75¢ per book in Canada.* I understand that accepting the 2 free books and gifts places me under no obligation to buy anything. I can always return a shipment and cancel at any time. Even if I never buy another book, the two free books and gifts are mine to keep forever.

154/354 HDN F4YN

Name	(PLEASE PRINT)	
Address		Apt. #
City	State/Prov.	Zip/Postal Code

Signature (if under 18, a parent or guardian must sign)

Mail to the **Harlequin® Reader Service:**
IN U.S.A.: P.O. Box 1867, Buffalo, NY 14240-1867
IN CANADA: P.O. Box 609, Fort Erie, Ontario L2A 5X3

Want to try two free books from another line?
Call 1-800-873-8635 or visit www.ReaderService.com.

* Terms and prices subject to change without notice. Prices do not include applicable taxes. Sales tax applicable in N.Y. Canadian residents will be charged applicable taxes. Offer not valid in Quebec. This offer is limited to one order per household. Not valid for current subscribers to Harlequin American Romance books. All orders subject to credit approval. Credit or debit balances in a customer's account(s) may be offset by any other outstanding balance owed by or to the customer. Please allow 4 to 6 weeks for delivery. Offer available while quantities last.

Your Privacy—The Harlequin® Reader Service is committed to protecting your privacy. Our Privacy Policy is available online at www.ReaderService.com or upon request from the Harlequin Reader Service.

We make a portion of our mailing list available to reputable third parties that offer products we believe may interest you. If you prefer that we not exchange your name with third parties, or if you wish to clarify or modify your communication preferences, please visit us at www.ReaderService.com/consumerschoice or write to us at Harlequin Reader Service Preference Service, P.O. Box 9062, Buffalo, NY 14269. Include your complete name and address.

HAR13R

Will Cash pulled off the road and parked next to the
mailbox at the entrance to the family farm. As usual the
box was stuffed. He gathered the envelopes and hopped
into the truck, then directed the air vents toward his face.
Normal highs for June were in the low nineties, but today's
temperature hovered near one hundred, promising a long
hot summer for southwest Arizona.

He sifted through the pile. Grocery store ads, business
flyers, electric bill. His fingers froze on a letter addressed to
Willie Nelson Cash. He didn't recognize the feminine script
and there was no return address. Before he could examine the
envelope further, his cell phone rang.

"Hold your horses, Porter. I'll be there in a minute."
Wednesday night was poker night, and his brothers and
brother-in-law were waiting for him in the bunkhouse. If not
for the weekly card game, they'd hardly see each other.

He tossed the mail aside and drove on. After parking in
the yard, he walked over to the bunkhouse, opening the letter
addressed to him. When he removed the note inside, a photo
fell out and landed on his boot. He snatched it off the ground
and stared at the image.

What the heck?

Dear Will… He read a few more lines, but the words blurred and a loud buzzing filled his ears. The kid in the picture was named Ryan and he was fourteen years old.

Slowly Will's eyes focused and he studied the photo. The young man had the same brownish-blond hair as Will did, but his eyes weren't brown—they were blue like his mother's.

"Buck!" he shouted. "Get your butt out here right now!"

When Buck came out, the rest of the Cash brothers and their brother-in-law, Gavin, followed.

"What's wrong?" Johnny's blue eyes darkened with concern.

Will ignored his eldest brother and waved the letter at Buck. "You knew all along."

Buck stepped forward. "Knew what?"

"Remember Marsha Bugler?"

"Sure. Why?"

"She said you'd vouch for her that she's telling the truth."

His brother's eye twitched—a sure sign of guilt. "The truth about what?"

"That after I got her pregnant, she kept the baby."

The color drained from Buck's face.

The tenuous hold Will had on his temper broke. "You've kept in touch with Marsha since high school. How the hell could you not tell me that I had a son!"

Look for HER SECRET COWBOY,
the next exciting title in The Cash Brothers *miniseries,*
next month from Marin Thomas

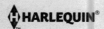
HARLEQUIN®

American Romance®

Can't get enough of those Cadence Creek Cowboys?

Coming soon from
New York Times bestselling author

Donna Alward

HER RANCHER RESCUER

Businessman-turned-rancher Jack Shepard's been burned before. He'll be damned if he'll let vivacious Amy Wilson past his defenses! Except beneath the bubbly exterior lies a beautiful, warmhearted woman he can't resist....

Available February 2014, from
Harlequin American Romance

Wherever books and ebooks are sold!